Ronald Knox and The Murder Room

》》 This title is part of The Murder Room, our series dedicated to making available out-of-print or hard-to-find titles by classic crime writers.

Crime fiction has always held up a mirror to society. The Victorians were fascinated by sensational murder and the emerging science of detection; now we are obsessed with the forensic detail of violent death. And no other genre has so captivated and enthralled readers.

Vast troves of classic crime writing have for a long time been unavailable to all but the most dedicated frequenters of second-hand bookshops. The advent of digital publishing means that we are now able to bring you the backlists of a huge range of titles by classic and contemporary crime writers, some of which have been out of print for decades.

From the genteel amateur private eyes of the Golden Age and the femmes fatales of pulp fiction, to the morally ambiguous hard-boiled detectives of mid twentieth-century America and their descendants who walk our twenty-first century streets, The Murder Room has it all. **》》**

The Murder Room
Where Criminal Minds Meet

themurderroom.com

Ronald Arbuthnott Knox (1888–1957)

It was Ronald Knox, who, as a pioneer of Golden Age detective fiction, codified the rules of the genre in his 'Ten Commandments of Detection', which stipulated, among other rules, that 'No Chinaman must figure in the story', and 'Not more than one secret room or passage is allowable'. He was a Sherlock Holmes aficionado, writing a satirical essay that was read by Arthur Conan Doyle himself, and is credited with creating the notion of 'Sherlockian studies', which treats Sherlock Holmes as a real-life character. Educated at Eton and Oxford, Knox was ordained as priest in the Church of England but later entered the Roman Catholic Church. He completed the first Roman Catholic translation of the Bible into English for more than 350 years, and wrote detective stories in order to supplement the modest stipend of his Oxford Chaplaincy.

The Viaduct Murder
The Three Taps
The Footsteps at the Lock
The Body in the Silo
Still Dead
Double Cross Purposes

The Three Taps

Ronald Knox

An Orion book

Copyright © Lady Magdalen Asquith 1927

The right of Ronald Knox to be identified as the author of this work
has been asserted in accordance with the Copyright, Designs and
Patents Act 1988.

This edition published by
The Orion Publishing Group Ltd
Orion House
5 Upper St Martin's Lane
London WC2H 9EA

An Hachette UK company
A CIP catalogue record for this book is available from the British Library

ISBN 978 1 4719 0055 6

www.orionbooks.co.uk

Printed and bound by CPI Group (UK) Ltd, Croydon, CR0 4YY

Dedicated to Susan and Francis Baker
Only he mustn't sit up too late over it.

CONTENTS

1. *The Euthanasia Policy*   1
2. *The Detective Malgré Lui*   9
3. *At the 'Load of Mischief'*   16
4. *The Bedroom*   23
5. *Supper, and Mr Brinkman*   30
6. *An Ear at the Keyhole*   37
7. *From Leyland's Note-book*   44
8. *The Bishop at Home*   49
9. *The Late Rector of Hipley*   58
10. *The Bet Doubled*   65
11. *The Generalship of Angela*   76
12. *The Makings of a Trap*   83
13. *A Morning with the Haberdasher*   90
14. *Bredon is Taken for a Walk*   98
15. *A Scrap of Paper*   106
16. *A Visitor from Pullford*   113
17. *Mysterious Behaviour of the Old Gentleman*   120
18. *The Barmaid is Brought to Book*   127
19. *How Leyland Spent the Evening*   135
20. *How Bredon Spent the Evening*   142
21. *How Eames Spent the Evening*   148
22. *At a Standstill*   153
23. *Leyland's Account of it all*   166
24. *Mottram's Account of it all*   159
25. *Bredon's Account of it all*   173

CHAPTER I

The Euthanasia Policy

THE principles of insurance, they tell us, were not hidden from our Anglo-Saxon forefathers. How anybody had the enterprise, in those rough-and-tumble days, to guarantee a client against 'fire, water, robbery, or other calamity', remains a problem for the historian; the more so as it appears that mathematical calculations were first applied to the business by the eminent John de Witt. In our own time, at any rate, the insurance companies have woven a golden net under the tight-rope walk of existence; if life is a lottery, the prudent citizen faces it with the consciousness that he is backed both ways. Had the idea been thoroughly grasped in that remoter period, no doubt but Alfred's hostess would have been easily consoled for the damage done to her cakes, and King John handsomely compensated for all that he lost in the Wash. Let us thank the soaring genius of the human mind, which has thus found a means to canalize for us the waters of affliction; and let us always be scrupulous in paying up our premiums before the date indicated on the printed card, lest calamity should come upon us and find us unprepared.

In a sense, though, insurance was but an empirical science until the Indescribable Company made its appearance. The man who is insured with the Indescribable walks the world in armour of proof; those contrary accidents and mortifications which are a source of spiritual profit to the saint are a source of material advantage to him. No east wind but flatters him with the prospect of a lucrative cold; no dropped banana-skin but may suddenly hurl him into affluence. The chicken-farmer whose hen-houses are fitted with the Company's patent automatic egg-register can never make a failure of his business. The egg is no sooner laid than it falls gently through a slot, which marks its passage on a kind of taximeter; and if the total of eggs at the end of the month is below the average, the Company pays – I had almost said, the Company lays

1

– an exact monetary equivalent for the shortage. The Company, which thus takes upon itself the office of a hen, is equally ready, when occasion arises, to masquerade as a bee; if your hives are opened in the presence of its representative, you can distend every empty cell with sweet nectar at the Company's expense. Doctors can guarantee themselves against an excess of panel patients, barristers against an absence of briefs. You can insure every step you take on this side of the grave, but no one of them on such handsome terms as the step which takes you into the grave; and it is confidently believed that, if certain practical difficulties could be got over, the Indescribable would somehow contrive to frank your passage into the world beyond. Wags have made merry at the Company's expense, alleging that a burglar can insure himself against a haul of sham jewels, and a clergyman against insufficient attendance at evensong. They tell stories of a client who murmured 'Thank God!' as he fell down a liftshaft, and a shipwrecked passenger who manifested the liveliest annoyance at the promptness of his rescuers when he was being paid for floating in a life-belt at the rate of ten pounds a minute. So thoroughly has the Indescribable reversed our scale of values here below.

But of all the Company's enterprises none can rival, in importance or in popularity, the so-called Euthanasia policy. One of the giant brains that organize the undertaking observed with compassion the doubtful lot of human kind, which makes the business man sweat and labour and agonize, uncertain whether he himself will reap the fruits of his industry, or whether they will pass to an heir in whom, on the whole, he is less interested. It follows, of course, from the actuarial point of view that he needs a policy which covers both possibilities, immature death or unexpected longevity, but the former on a more princely scale than the latter. If you take out a Euthanasia policy, you will pay very heavy premiums; that goes without saying. But you pay them with a sense of absolute security. If you should die before the age of sixty-five, a fortune is immediately distributed to your heirs and assigns. If you outlive that crucial age, you become thenceforward, until the decree of nature takes its tardy effect, the pensioner of the Company; every faltering breath you draw, in the last stages of senility, is money to you; your heirs and assigns, instead of looking forward heartlessly to the moment of your release, conspire to keep your body and soul together with every known artifice of modern medicine – it is in their interest to do so. There is but one way in which you can forfeit the manifest advantages of the scheme, and that is self-murder. So complex is our human fashioning that men may even be tempted to enrich their surviving relatives by such means; and you will find, accordingly, at the bottom of your Euthanasia policy, an ominous black hand directing attention to the fact that in the event of suicide, no benefits are legally recoverable.

It goes without saying that the Indescribable Buildings are among the finest in London. It appears to be an axiom with those who conduct business in the modern or American manner, that efficiency is impossible unless all your transactions are conducted in an edifice not much smaller and not much less elaborate than the Taj Mahal. Why this should be so, it is difficult to explain. In a less credulous age, we might have been tempted to wonder where all the money came from; whether (to put it brutally) our premiums might not have worked out a little lower if the company's premises had not been quite so high. After all, our solicitor lives in horrid, dingy little chambers, with worn-out carpets and immemorial cobwebs on the wall – does he never feel that this squalor will fail to inspire confidence? Apparently not; yet the modern insurance company must impress us all, through the palatial splendour of its offices, with the idea that there is a vast reserve of capital behind it. The wildest voluptuousness of an eastern tyrant is less magnificent in its architectural schemes than the hard-headed efficiency of the American business man. Chatting in the waiting-room of some such edifice, Sardanapalus might have protested that it beat him how they did it, and Kubla Khan might have registered the complaint that it was all very well, but the place didn't feel homey.

Indescribable House is an enormously high building, with long, narrow windows that make it look like an

Egyptian tomb. It is of white stone, of course, so time-defying in its appearance that it seems almost blasphemous to remember the days when it was simply a gigantic shell composed of iron girders. Over the front door there is a group of figures in relief, more than life-size; the subject is intended, I believe, to be Munificence wiping away the tears of Widowhood, though the profane have identified it before now as Uncle Sam picking Britannia's pocket. This is continued all round the four sides by a frieze, ingeniously calculated to remind the spectator of the numerous risks which mortality has to run; here is a motor-accident, with an ambulance carrying off the injured parties; here an unmistakable shipwreck; there a big-game hunter is being gored by a determined-looking buffalo, while a lion prowls thoughtfully in the background. Of the interior I cannot speak so positively, for even those who are favoured enough to be the Company's clients never seem to go up beyond the fourth floor. But rumour insists that there is a billiard-room for the convenience of the directors, who never go there; and that from an aeroplane, in hot weather, you can see the clerks playing tennis on the roof. What they do when they are not playing tennis, or what possible use there can be in all those multitudinous rooms on the fifth, sixth, and seventh floors, is a thought that paralyses the imagination.

In one of the waiting-rooms on the ground floor, sitting under a large palm-tree and reading a closely-reasoned article in the *Actuaries' and Bottomry Gazette*, sat a client to whom the reader will do well to direct attention, for our story is concerned with him. His look, his dress, his manner betrayed the rich man only to those who have frequented the smaller provincial towns and know how little, in those centres, money has to do with education. He had a short black coat with very broad and long lapels, a starched collar that hesitated between the Shakespeare and the all-the-way-and-back-again patterns, a double-breasted waistcoat from which hung a variety of seals, lockets, and charms – in London, in fact, you would have put him down for an old-fashioned bank cashier with a moderate income. Actually, he could have bought you out of your present job at double the salary, and hardly felt it. In Pullford, a large Midland town, which you will probably never visit, men nudged one another and pointed to him as one of the wealthiest residents. In the ante-room of the Indescribable Office he looked, and perhaps felt, like a school-boy waiting his turn for pocket-money. Yet even here he was a figure recognizable to the attendant who stood there smoothing out back numbers of the *Actuaries' and Bottomry Gazette*. For this man, called Mottram by accident of birth and Jephthah through the bad taste of his parents, was the holder of a Euthanasia policy.

Another attendant approached him, summoning him to his appointed interview. There was none of that 'Mr Mottram, please!' which reverberates so grimly through the dentist's waiting room. At the Indescribable, the attendants come up close to you and beckon you away with confidential whispers; it is part of the tradition. Mr Mottram rose, and was gently sucked up by the lift on to the second floor, where fresh attendants ushered him on into one of the few rooms that really mattered. Here he was met by a pleasant, rather languid young man, delicately dressed, University-bred, whose position in the complicated hierarchy of the Indescribable it is no business of ours to determine.

'How do you do, Mr Mottram? Keeping well, I hope?'

Mr Mottram had the blunt manner of his fellow-towns-men, and did not appreciate the finesse of Metropolitan conversational openings. 'Ah, that's right,' he said; 'best for you I should keep well, eh? You and I won't quarrel there. Well, it may surprise you, but it's my health I've come to talk about. I don't look ill, do I?'

'You look fit for anything. I'd sooner be your insurance agent than your family doctor, Mr Mottram.' The young man was beginning to pick up the Pullford idea of light small talk.

'Fit for anything, that's right. And, mind you, I feel fit for anything. Never felt better. Two years!'

'I beg your pardon?'

'Two years, that's what he says. What's the good of being able to know about these things if they can't do anything *for* 'em, that's what I want to know? And mind you, he says there isn't anything for it, not in the long run.

5

He tells me to take this and that, you know, and give up this and that –'

'I'm sorry, Mr Mottram, but I don't quite understand. Is this your doctor you're talking about?'

'No doctor of mine. My doctor down in Pullford, he couldn't tell what was the matter. Sent me on to this big man in London I've been seeing this morning. Two years, he says. Seems hard, doesn't it?'

'Oh... You've been to a specialist. I say, I'm most awfully sorry.' The young man was quite serious in his condolences, though he was even more embarrassed than actually grieved. It seemed horrible to him that this red-faced man who looked so well and obviously enjoyed his meals should be going where Numa and Ancus went before him; he did not fit into the picture. No taint of professionalism entered into this immediate reaction. But Mr Mottram still took the business line.

'Ah! sorry – you may say that. It may mean half a million to you, mayn't it?'

'Yes, but look here, these specialists are often wrong. Famous case of one who went potty and told all his patients they were for it. Look here, what about seeing our man? He'd vet you, gladly.'

It need hardly be said that the Indescribable keeps its own private physician, whose verdict must be obtained before any important insurance is effected. He is consider-ed to be one of the three best doctors in England, and fantastic stories are told about the retaining fee which induced him to give up his practice in Harley Street. Once more, the young man was entirely disinterested; once more, Mr Mottram saw ground for suspicion. It looked to him as if the Company were determined to get stable information about the exact state of his health, and he did not like the idea.

'It's of no consequence, thank you all the same. It isn't as if my case was a doubtful one; I can give you the doctor's certificate if needed. But I didn't come here to talk about that; I came on business. You know how I stand?'

The young man had just been looking up Mr Mott-ram's docket, and knew all about him well enough. But the Indescribable cultivates the family touch; it likes to treat its clients as man to man, not as so many 'lives'. 'Let's see' – the young man appeared to be dragging the depths of memory – 'you should be sixty-three now, eh? And in two years' time – why, it looks as if it were just touch and go whether your policy covered a case of, h'm, premature decease or not, doesn't it?'

'That's right. My birthday's in a fortnight's time, more or less. If that doctor was dead accurate, it'll stand you in five hundred thousand. If he put the date a bit too soon, then I get nothing, and you pay nothing; that's how it is, isn't it?'

'Looks like it, I'm afraid. Of course, you'll understand, Mr Mottram, the Company has to work by rule of thumb in these cases.'

'I see that. But, look at it this way. When I took out that policy, I wasn't thinking much of the insurance part; I've no kith nor kin except one nephew, and he's seen fit to quarrel with me, so nothing goes to him, anyhow. If that half-million falls in, it will just go to charity. But what I'd set my heart on was the annuity; we're a long-lived family, mostly, and I'd looked forward to spending my last days in comfort, d'you see? Well, there's no chance of that, after what the doctor's been telling me. So I don't value that Youth in Asia policy as much as I did, see? And I've come here to make you a fair offer.'

'The Company –' began the young man.

'Let me have my say, and you shall have yours afterwards. They call me rich, and I suppose I am rich: but my stuff is tied up more than you'd think; with money as tight as it is, you can't just sell out of a thing when you feel inclined. What I want is ready money – doctor's bills, you know, and foreign travel, and treatment, and that. So this is my offer – you pay back half the premiums from the time I started insuring with you, half the premiums, mind you; and if I die before I reach sixty-five, then we call it off; you pay no insurance: if I live beyond sixty-five, we call it off, and you pay no annuity. Come now, there's a business offer. What do you people say to it?'

'I'm sorry; I'm frightfully sorry. But, you know, we've had this kind of offer before, and the Company has always

7

taken the line that it can't go back on the original contract. If we lose, we lose; if the client loses, he must shoulder the responsibility. If we once went in for cancelling our insurances like that, our whole credit would suffer. I know you mean well by us, Mr Mottram, and we're grateful to you for the generosity of the offer; but it can't be done; really it can't.'

There was a heavy silence for nearly a minute. Then Mr Mottram, pathetic in his disappointment, tried his last card.

'You could put it to the directors, couldn't you? Stands to reason you couldn't accept an offer of that kind without referring it to them. But you could put it to them at their next meeting, eh?'

'I could put it to the directors; indeed, I will. But I'm sorry to say I can't hold out any hopes. The premium of the Euthanasia policy is so stiff that we're always having people wanting to back out of it half-way, but the directors have never consented. If you take my advice, Mr Mottram, you'll take a second opinion about your health, go carefully this next year or two, and live to enjoy that annuity – for many years, I hope.' The young man, after all, was a paid official; he did not stand to lose.

Mr Mottram rose; he declined all offers of refreshment. A little wearily, yet holding his head high, he let the confidential attendants usher him out. The young man made some notes, and the grim business of the Indescribable Company went on. In distant places, ships were foundering, factories were being struck by lightning, crops were being spoiled by blight, savages were raiding the peaceful country-side, men were lying on air-cushions, fighting for breath in the last struggle of all. And to the Indescribable Company all these things meant business; most of them meant loss. But the loss never threatened their solvency for a moment; the law of averages saw to that.

CHAPTER 2

The Detective Malgré Lui

I HAVE already mentioned that the Indescribable kept its own tame doctor, a man at the very head of his profession. He was not in the least necessary to it; that is to say, a far cheaper man would have done the work equally well. But it suited the style of the Indescribable to have the very best man, and to advertise the fact that he had given up his practice in order to work exclusively for the Company; it was all of a piece with the huge white building, and the frieze, and the palms in the waiting-room. It looked well. For a quite different reason the Indescribable retained its own private detective. This fact was not advertised; nor was he ever referred to in the official communications of the Company except as 'our representative'. He carried neither a lens nor a forceps – not even a revolver; he took no injections; he had no stupid confidential friend, but a private detective he was for all that. An amateur detective I will not call him, for the Company paid him, as you would expect, quite handsomely; but he had nothing whatever to do with Scotland Yard, where the umbrellas go to.

He was not an ornament to the company; he fulfilled a quite practical purpose. There are, even outside the humorous stories, business men in a small way who find it more lucrative to burn down their premises than to sell their stock. There are ladies – ladies whose name the Indescribable would never dream of giving away – who pawn their jewels, buy sham ones, and then try to make the original insurance policy cover them in the event of theft. There are small companies (believe it or not) who declare an annual loss by selling their stuff below cost price to themselves under another name. Such people flocked to the Indescribable. It was so vast a concern that you felt no human pity about robbing it – it was like cheating the income-tax, and we all know what some people feel about that. The Indescribable never prose-

9

cuted for fraud; instead, it allowed a substantial margin for these depredations, which it allowed to continue. But where shady work was suspected, 'our representative' would drop in, in the most natural way in the world; and, by dint of some searching inquiries, made while the delinquent's back was turned, would occasionally succeed in showing up a fraud, and saving the company a few hundreds of thousands by doing so.

The Company's representative, and our hero, was Miles Bredon, a big, good-humoured, slightly lethargic creature still in the early thirties. His father had been a lawyer of moderate eminence and success. When Miles went to school, it was quite clear that he would have to make his own way in the world, and very obscure how he was going to do it. He was not lazy, exactly, but he was the victim of hobbies which perpetually diverted his attention. He was a really good mathematician, for example; but as he never left a sum unfinished and 'went on to the next', his marks never did him justice. He was a good cross-country runner; but in the middle of a run he would usually catch sight of some distraction which made him wander three miles out of his course and come in last. It was his nature to be in love with the next thing he had to do, to shrink in loathing from the mere thought of the next but one. The war came in time to solve the problem of his career; more fortunate than some, he managed to hit on a *métier* in the course of it. He became intelligence officer; did well, then did brilliantly; was mentioned in despatches, though not decorated. What was more to the point, his Colonel happened to be a friend of some minor director of the Indescribable, and, hearing that a discreet man was needed to undertake the duties outlined above, recommended Bredon. The offer fell at his feet just when he was demobilized; he hated the idea of it, but was sensible enough to realize, even then, that ex-officers cannot be choosers. He was accepted on his own terms, namely that he should not have to sit in an office kicking his heels; he would always be at home, and the Company might call him in when he was wanted.

In a few years he had made himself indispensable to his employers – that is to say, they thought they could not

get on without him, though in fact his application to his
duties was uncertain and desultory. Four out of five inquiries meant nothing to him; he made nothing of them,
and Whitechapel thanked the God of its father's for his in-
competence. The fifth case would appeal to his capricious
imagination; he would be prodigal of time and of pains,
and bring off some *coup* which was hymned for weeks,
behind closed doors, in the Indescribable Buildings. There
was that young fellow at Croydon, for example, who had
his motor-bicycle insured, but not his mother-in-law. Her
body was found at the foot of an embankment beside a
lonely road in Kent, and there was no doubt that it had
been shot out of the side-car; only (as Bredon managed to
prove) the lady's death had occurred on the previous day,
from natural causes. There was the well-known bootlegger
– well known, at least, to the U.S. police – who insured all
his cargoes with the Indescribable, and then laid secret
information against himself, whereby vigilant officials
sank hundreds of dummy cases in the sea, all the bottles
containing sea-water. And there was the lady of fashion
who burgled her own jewels in the most plausible manner
you could imagine, and had them sold in Paris. These
crooked ways, too, the fitful intuitions of Miles Bredon
made plain in the proper quarters.

He was well thought of, in fact, by everyone except himself. For himself, he bitterly regretted the necessity that
had made him become a spy – he would use no other
word for it, and constantly alarmed his friends by announcing his intention of going into the publishing trade,
or doing something relatively honest. The influence which
saved him on these occasions was that of – how shall I say
it? – his wife. I know – I know it is quite wrong to have
your detective married until the last chapter. But it is not
my fault. It is the fault of two mocking eyes and two very
capable hands that were employed in driving brass-hats
to and fro in London at the end of the war. Bredon sur-
rendered to these, and made a hasty but singularly fortunate marriage. Angela Bredon was under no illusions about
the splendid figure in khaki that stood beside her at the
altar. Wiser than her generation, she realized that marri-
ages were not 'for the duration'; that she would have to

11

spend the rest of her life with a large, untidy, absent-minded man who would frequently forget that she was in the room. She saw that he needed above all things a nurse and a chauffeur, and she knew that she could supply both these deficiencies admirably. She took him as a husband, with all a husband's failings, and the Indescribable itself could not have guaranteed her more surely against the future.

There is a story of some Bishop or important person who got his way at Rome rather unexpectedly over an appeal, and, when asked by his friends how he did it, replied, *Fallendo Infallibilem.* It might have been the motto of Angela's mastery over her husband; the detective, always awake to the possibilities of fraudulent dealing in every other human creature, did not realize that his wife was a tiny bit cleverer than he was, and was always conspiring for his happiness behind his back. For instance, it was his custom of an evening to play a very long and complicated game of patience, which he had invented for himself; you had to use four packs, and the possible permutations of it were almost unlimited. It was an understood thing in the household that Angela, although she had grasped the rules of the game, did not really know how to play it. But when, as often happened, the unfinished game had to be left undisturbed all night, she was quite capable of stealing down early in the morning and altering the positions of one or two cards, so that he should get the game 'out' in time to cope with his ordinary work. These pious deceits of hers were never, I am glad to say, unmasked.

About a fortnight after Mr Mottram's interview with the young man at Indescribable House, these two fortunate people were alone together after dinner; she alternately darning socks and scratching the back of a sentimental-looking fox-terrier; he playing his interminable patience. The bulk of the pack lay on a wide table in front of him, but there were outlying sections of the design dotted here and there on the floor within reach of his hand. When the telephone bell rang, he looked up at her appealingly; obviously, he was tied hand and foot by his occupation – to her, it only meant putting her darning away,

taking the fox-terrier off her feet, and going out into the
hall. She understood the signal, and obeyed it. There was
a fixed law of the household that if she answered a call
which was meant for him, he must try to guess what it was
about before she told him. This was good for him, she
said; it developed the sleuth instinct.

'Hullo! Mrs Bredon speaking – who is it, please? ...Oh,
it's you... Yes, he's in, but he's not answering the tele-
phone... No, only drunk...Just rather drunk... Business?
Good; that's just what he wants... A man called what?...
M-o-t-t-r-a-m, Mottram, yes... Never heard of it... St
William's? Oh, the MIDLANDS, that are sodden and un-
kind, that sort of Midlands, yes... Oh!... Is it – what?...
Is it supposed to have been an accident?... Oh, that
generally means suicide, doesn't it?... Staying where?...
Where's that?... All right, doesn't matter, I'll look it up...
At an inn? Oh, then it was in somebody else's bed really!
What name?... What a jolly name! Well, where's Miles
to go? To Chilthorpe?... Yes, rather, we can start bright
and early. Is it an important case? Is it an important
case?... Oo! I say! I wish I could get Miles to die and
leave me half a million! Right O, he'll wire you tomorrow... Yes, quite, thanks... Good night.'

'Interpret, please,' said Angela, returning to the draw-
ing-room. 'Why, you've been going on with your patience
the whole time! I suppose you didn't listen to a word I
was saying?'

'How often am I to tell you that the memory and the
attention function inversely? I remember all you said,
precisely because I wasn't paying attention to it. First of
all, it was Sholto, because he was ringing you up on
business, but it was somebody you know quite well – at
least, I hope you don't talk like that to the tradesmen.'

'Sholto, yes, ringing up from the office. He wanted to
talk to you.'

'So I gathered. Was it quite necessary to tell him I was
drunk?'

'Well, I couldn't think of anything else to say at the
moment. I couldn't tell him you were playing patience,
or he might have thought we were unhappily married. Go
on, Sherlock.'

'Mottram, living at some place in the Midlands you've never heard of, but staying at a place called Chilthorpe – he's died, and his death wants investigating; that's obvious.'

'How did you know he was dead?'

'From the way you said Oh – besides, you said he'd died in his bed, or implied it. And there's some question of half a million insurance – Euthanasia, I suppose? Really, the Euthanasia's been responsible for more crimes than psycho-analysis.'

'Yes, I'm afraid you've got it all right. What did he die of?'

'Something that generally means suicide – or rather you think it does. The old sleeping-draught business? Veronal?'

'No, stupid, gas. The gas left turned on. And where's Chilthorpe, please?'

'It's on the railway. If my memory serves me right, it is Chilthorpe and Gorrington, between Bull's Cross and Lowgill Junction. But the man, you say, belongs somewhere else?'

'Pullford, at least, it sounded like that. In the Midlands somewhere, he said.'

'Pullford, good Lord, yes. One of these frightful holes. They make perambulators or something there, don't they? A day's run, I should think, in the car. But of course it's this Chilthorpe place we want to get to. You wouldn't like to look it up in the Gazetteer while I just get this row finished, would you?'

'I shan't get your sock finished, then. On your own foot be it. Let's see, here's Pullford all right... It isn't perambulators they make, it's drain-pipes. There's a Grammar School there, and an asylum; and the Parish Church is a fine specimen of early Perp., extensively restored in 1842; they always are. Has been the seat of a R. Cath. bishopric since 1850. The Baptist chapel –'

'I did mention, didn't I, that it was Chilthorpe I wanted to know about?'

'All in good time. Let's see, Chilthorpe – it isn't a village really, it's a t'nship. It has 2,500 inhabitants. There's a lot here about the glebe. It stands on the river Busk, and there is trout fishing.'

14

'Ah, that sounds better.'

'Meaning exactly?'

'Well, it sounds as if the fellow had done himself in by accident all right. He went there to fish – you won't go to a strange village to commit suicide.'

'Unless you've got electric light in your house, and want to commit suicide with gas.'

'That's true. What was the name of the inn, by the way?'

'The "Load of Mischief". Such a jolly dedication, I think.'

'Now let's try the map.'

'I was coming to that. Here's the Busk all right. I say, how funny, there's a place on the Busk called Mottram.'

'Anywhere near Chilthorpe?'

'I haven't found it yet. Oh, yes, here it is, about four miles away. Incidentally, it's only twenty miles or so from Pullford. Well, what about it? Are we going by car?'

'Why not? The Rolls is in excellent condition. Two or three days ought to see us through; we can stay, with any luck, at the "Load of Mischief", and the youthful Francis will be all the better for being left to his nurse for a day or two. You've been feeding him corn, and he is becoming obstreperous.'

'You don't deserve to have a son. However, I think you're right. I don't want to trust you alone in a t'nship of 2,500 inhabitants, some of them female. Miles, dear, this is going to be one of your big successes, isn't it?'

'On the contrary, I shall lose no time in reporting to the Directors that the deceased gentleman had an unfortunate accident with the gas, and they had better pay up like sportsmen. I shall further point out that it is a great waste of their money keeping a private spy at all.'

'Good, then I'll divorce you. I'm going to bed now. Not beyond the end of that second row, mind; we shall have to make an early start tomorrow.'

CHAPTER 3

At the 'Load of Mischief'

By next morning, Bredon's spirits had risen. He had received, by the early post, a confidential letter from the Company describing Mr Mottram's curious offer, and suggesting (naturally) that the state of his health made suicide a plausible conjecture. The morning was fine, the car running well, the road they had selected in admirable condition. It was still before tea-time when they turned off from its excellent surface on to indifferent by-roads, through which they had to thread their way with difficulty. The sign-posts, as is the wont of English sign-posts, now blazoned Chilthorpe, Chilthorpe, Chilthorpe, as if it were the lodestone of the neighbourhood, now passed it over in severe silence, preferring to call attention to the fact that you were within five furlongs of Little Stubley. They had fallen, besides, upon hill-country, with unexpected turns and precipitous gradients; they followed, with enforced windings, the bleak valley of the Busk, which swirled beneath them over smooth boulders between desolate banks. It was just after they had refused the fifth invitation to Little Stubley that the County Council's arrangements played them false; there was a clear issue between two rival roads, with no trace of a sign-post to direct their preference. It was here that they saw, and hailed, an old gentleman who was making casts into a promising pool about twenty yards away.

'Chilthorpe?' said the old gentleman. 'All the world seems to be coming to Chilthorpe. The County Council does not appear to have allowed for the possibility of its becoming such a centre of fashion. If you are fond of scenery, you should take the road to the left; it goes over the hill. If you like your tea weak, you had better take the valley road to the right. Five o'clock is tea-time at the "Load of Mischief", and there is no second brew.'

Something in the old gentleman's tone seemed to invite confidences. 'Thank you very much,' said Bredon. 'I suppose the "Load of Mischief" is the only inn that one can stop at?'

'There was never much to be said for the "Swan". But today the "Load of Mischief" has added to its attractions; it is not everywhere you can sleep with the corpse of a suicide in the next room. And the police are in the house, to satisfy the most morbid imagination.'

'The police? When did they come?'

'About luncheon-time. They are understood to have a clue. I am only afraid, myself, that they will want to drag the river. The police always drag the river if they can think of nothing else to do.'

'You're staying at the inn, I gather?'

'I am the surviving guest. When you have tasted the coffee in the morning, you will understand the temptation to suicide, but so far I have resisted it. You are not re- latives, I hope, of the deceased?'

'No; I'm from the Indescribable. We insured him, you know.'

'It must be a privilege to die under such auspices. But I am afraid I have gone beyond my book; when I say poor Mottram committed suicide, I am giving you theory, not fact.'

'The police theory?'

'Hardly. I left before they arrived. It is the landlady's theory, and when you know her better, you will know that it is as well not to disagree with her; it provokes discussion.'

'I am afraid she must be very much worried by all this.'

'She is in the seventh heaven of lamentation. You could knock her down, she tells me, with a feather. She insists that her custom is ruined for ever; actually, you are the second party to stay at the inn as the result of this affair, and the jug and bottle business at mid-day was something incredible. The Band of Hope was there *en masse*, swilling beer in the hope of picking up some gossip.'

'The other party, were they relations?'

'Oh, no, it's a policeman; a real policeman from London. The secretary, I suppose, must have lost his head, and insisted on making a *cause célèbre* of the thing. I forgot him, by the way, a little chap called Brinkman; he's at the "Load", too. A thousand pardons, but I see a fish rising.

17

It is so rare an event here that I must go and attend to it.'
And, nodding pleasantly, the old gentleman made his way
to the bank again.

Chilthorpe is a long, straggling village, with the business
part (such as it is) at the lower end. The Church is there,
and the 'Load of Mischief', and a few shops; here too, the
Busk flows under a wide stone bridge – a performance
which, at most times of the day, attracts a fair crowd of
local spectators. The houses are of grey stone, the roofs
of blue slate. The rest of the village climbs úp along the
valley, all in one street; the houses stand perched on the
edge of a steep slope, too steep, almost, for the cultivation
of gardens, though a few currant and gooseberry bushes
retain a precarious foothold. The view has its charms;
when mists hang over it in autumn, or when the smoke of
the chimneys lingers idly on a still summer evening, it has
a mysterious and strangely un-English aspect.

The hostess, presumably to be identified with J. Davis,
licensed to sell wines, spirits, and tobacco, met them on
the threshold, voluble and apparently discouraging. Her
idea seemed to be that she could not have any more guests
coming and committing suicide in her house. Bredon,
afraid that his patience or his gravity would break down,
put Angela in charge of the conversation; so delicate was
her tact, so well-placed her sympathy, that within ten
minutes their arrival was being hailed as a godsend, and
Mrs Davis, ordering the barmaid to bring tea as soon as it
could be procured, ushered them into a private room,
assuring them of accommodation upstairs, when she could
put things to rights. It had been one thing after another,
she complained, all day, she didn't really hardly know
which way to turn, and her house always a respectable
one. There was not much custom, it seemed, at Chilthorpe,
lying so far away from the main road and that – you
would have supposed that in an R.A. listed hotel suicides
were a matter of daily occurrence, and the management
knew how to deal with them. Whereas Mrs Davis hadn't
anybody not but the girl and the Boots, and him only with
one arm. And those boys coming and looking in through
the front window, disgraceful, she called it, and what
were the police for if they couldn't put a stop to it? And

the reporters – six of them she'd turned away that very day, coming and prying into what didn't concern them. They didn't get a word out of her, that was one thing.

Though, mark you, if Mrs Davis didn't know poor Mr Mottram, who did? Coming there regular year after year for the fishing, poor gentleman; such a quiet gentleman, too, and never any goings-on. And how was she to know what would come of it? It wasn't that the gas leaked; time and again she'd had those pipes seen to, and no complaints made. If there had have been anything wrong, Mr Pulteney he'd have let her hear about it, he was one for having everything just as he liked, and no mistake. ... Yes, that would be him, he was a great one for the fishing. Such a queer gentleman, too, and always taking you up short. Why, yesterday morning, when she went to tell him about what had happened in the night, he was as cool as anything; all he said was, 'In that case, Mrs Davis, I will fish the Long Pool this morning,' like that he said. Whereas Mr Brinkman, that was the secretary, he was in a great taking about it, didn't hardly know what he said or did, Mr Brinkman didn't. And to think of all the gas that was wasted; on all night it was, and who was to pay for it was more than she knew. Summing up, Mrs Davis was understood to observe that it was a world for sorrow, and man was cut down like a flower, as the sparks fly upwards. However, there was Them above as knew, and what would be would be.

Of all this diatribe Bredon was a somewhat languid auditor. He recognized the type too well to suppose that any end was to be gained by cross-examination. Angela cooed and sighed, and dabbed her eyes now and again at appropriate moments, and in so doing won golden opinions from the tyrannous conversationalist. It was a strong contrast when the maid came in with the tea-things; she plumped them down in silence, tossing her head defiantly, as who should imply that somebody had recently found fault with her behind the scenes, but she was not going to take any notice of it. She was a strapping girl, of undeniable good looks, spoilt (improved, the Latins would have said) by a slight cast in one eye. In the absence of any very formidable competition, it was easy to imagine her the belle of the village. So resolute did her taciturnity appear that even Angela, who could draw confidences from a stone, instinctively decided that it would be best to question her later on. Instead, she whiled away the interminable interval which separates the arrival of the milk-jug from that of the tea-pot by idly turning over the leaves of the old-fashioned visitors' book. The Misses Harrison, it appeared, had received every attention from their kind and considerate hostess. The Pullford Cycling Club had met for their annual outing, and pronounced themselves 'full to bursting, and coming back next year'. An obvious newly-married couple had found the neighbourhood very quiet; a subsequent annotator had added the words 'I don't think', with several marks of exclamation. The Wotherspoon family, a large one, testified to having had a rattling good time at this old-world hostelry. The Reverend Arthur and Mrs Stump would carry away many pleasant memories of Chilthorpe and its neighbourhood.

Miles was wandering aimlessly about the room, inspecting those art treasures which stamp, invariably and unmistakably, the best room of a small country inn. There was the piano, badly out of tune, with a promiscuous heap of Dissenting hymn-books and forgotten dance tunes reposing on it. There were the two pictures which represent a lovers' quarrel and a lovers' reconciliation, the hero and heroine being portrayed in riding costume. There was a small bookshelf, full of Sunday-school prizes, interspersed with one or two advanced novels in cheap editions, left behind, clearly, by earlier visitors. There was a picture of Bournemouth in a frame of repulsive shells. There was a photograph of some local squire or other, on horseback. There were several portraits which were intended to perpetuate the memory of the late Mr Davis, a man of full bodily habit, whose clothes, especially his collar, seemed too tight for him. There were a couple of young gentlemen in khaki on the mantelpiece; there was a sailor, probably the one who had collected the strange assortment of picture post-cards in the album under the occasional table; there were three wedding groups, all apparently in the family – in a word, a detective interested in such problems might have read here, in picture, the incredibly long and complicated annals of the poor.

To Bredon it was all a matter of intense irritation. He was fond, when he visited the scene of some crime or some problem, of poking his way round the furniture, trying to pick up hints, from the books and the knick-knacks, about the character of the people he was dealing with. At least, he would say, if you cannot pick up evidence about them, you can always catch something of their atmosphere. Mottram had hardly played the game when he died in a country inn, where he had not been able to impress his surroundings with any touch of his own quality; this inn parlour was like any other inn parlour, and the dead body upstairs would be a problem in isolation, torn away from its proper context. The bedroom, doubtless, would have a text over the washing-stand, a large wardrobe stuffed with family clothes and moth-balls, a cheap print of the Soul's Awakening; it would just be an inn bedroom, there would be no Mottram about it.

'I say,' Angela interrupted suddenly, 'Mottram seems to have visited this place pretty regularly, and always for the fishing season. There are some fine specimens of his signature; the last only written two days ago.'

'Eh? What's that?' said Bredon. 'Written his signature in already, had he? Any date to it?'

'Yes, here it is, J. W. Mottram, June 13th to – and then a blank. He didn't know quite how long he would be staying, I suppose.'

'Let's see... Look here, that's all wrong, you know. This isn't a hotel register; it's just a Visitors' Book. And people who write in a Visitors' Book don't write till the day they leave.'

'Necessarily?'

'Invariably. Look here, look at Arthur Stump. You can see from his style and handwriting what a meticulous fellow he is. Well, he came here on May 21st, and stayed till May 26th. The Wilkinsons came here a day later, on the 22nd, and left on the 24th. But the Wilkinsons' entry comes first – that's because they left first, don't you see? And here is Violet Harris doing the same; she puts her name before the Sandeman party. Look at Mottram's entry last year. He didn't leave a blank then, and fill in his date of departure afterwards; you can always tell when a thing is filled in afterwards, because the spacing is never quite exact. No, Mottram did something quite foreign to his habit when he wrote June 13th to blank, and quite foreign to the habits of everyone I know.'

'You get these little ideas sometimes. No, you can't have tea till you come and sit at the table. I don't want you sloshing it about all over the place. Now, what can have been the idea of writing that entry? Nobody wanted proof that he'd been here. Could it be a forgery, done from last year's entry? That would mean that it isn't Mottram upstairs at all, really.'

'We shall know that soon enough... No, there's only one idea that seems to me to make sense. He came to this place knowing that he was never going to leave it alive. And consequently he wanted to put an entry in the book which would make it look as if he had been paying just an ordinary visit, and *was* expecting to leave it alive. People will never see that they're overreaching themselves when they do that kind of thing. It's absurd to go on such slight indications, but as far as I can see, the presumption is this – Mottram meant to commit suicide, and meant to make it look as if he hadn't.'

'The date's all right, I suppose?'

'Bound to be. No sense in falsifying it when it could always be verified from the bill. Landladies have a habit of knowing what night guests arrived.'

'Let's see, then; he arrived on the 13th; and he was found dead in the morning, that's yesterday morning, Tuesday. The 13th was Monday – he'd only been here one night.'

'Well, we'll hope we can find all that part out from the secretary. I don't much want another hour of Mrs Davis. Meanwhile, let's see if you can knock any more out of that tea-pot; I'm as thirsty as a fish.'

CHAPTER 4

The Bedroom

THEY did not escape another dose of Mrs Davis, who appeared soon afterwards to announce that the big upstairs room was ready for them, and would they step up and mind their heads, please, the stairs were that low. It was, indeed, a rambling sort of house, on three or four different levels, as country inns are wont to be; it did not seem possible to reach any one room from any other without going down and up again, or up and down again. At the head of the stairs Mrs Davis turned dramatically and pointed to a door marked 5. 'In there!' she said, the complicated emotion in her voice plainly indicating what was in there. To her obvious confusion the door opened as she spoke, and a little, dark man, whom they guessed then and knew afterwards to be the secretary, came out into the passage. He was followed by a policeman – no ingenuity could have doubted the fact – in plain clothes. Bredon's investigations were ordinarily made independently of, and for the most part unknown to, the official champions of justice. But on this occasion Fate had played into his hands. 'By Gad,' he cried, 'it's Leyland!'

It was, nor will I weary the reader by detailing the exclamations of surprise, the questionings, the reminiscences, the explanations which followed. Leyland had been an officer in the same battalion with Bredon for more than two years of the war; it was at a time when the authorities had perceived that there were not enough well-dressed young men in England to go round, and a police inspector who had already made a name for efficiency easily obtained commissioned rank; with equal ease he returned to the position of inspector when demobilized. Their memories of old comradeship promised to be so exhaustive and, to the lay mind, so exhausting, that Brinkman had gone downstairs and Angela Bredon to her room long before it was over; nay, Mrs Davis herself, outtalked for once, retired to her kitchen.

'Well, this is A1,' said Leyland at last. 'Sure to be left down here for a few days until I can clear things up a bit. And if you're working on the same lay, there's no reason why we should quarrel. Though I don't quite see what your people sent you down for, to start with.'

'Well, the man was very heavily insured, you know, and, for one reason or another, the Company were inclined to suspect suicide. Of course, if it's suicide, they don't pay up.'

'Well, you'd better lie low about it and stay on for a few days. Good for you and Mrs Bredon to get a bit of a holiday. But, of course, suicide is right off the map.'

'People do commit suicide, don't they, by leaving the gas on?'

'Yes, but they don't get up and turn the gas off, and then go back to bed to die. They don't open the window, and leave it open –'

'The gas turned off? The window opened? You don't mean –'

'I mean that if it was suicide it was a very rum kind of suicide, and if it was accident it was a very rum kind of accident. Mark you, I'm saying that to you, but don't you go putting it about the place. Some of these people in the inn may know more about it than they ought to. Mum's the word.'

'Yes, I can see that. Let's see, who were there in the house? This secretary fellow, and the old gentleman I saw down by the river, I suppose, and Mrs Davis and the barmaid and the Boots – that's all I've heard of up to date. That's right, keep 'em all under suspicion. But I wish you'd let me see the room. It seems to me there must be points of interest about it.'

'Best see it now, I think. They're going to fix up the corpse properly tonight; so far they've left things more or less untouched. There's just light enough left to have a look round.'

The inn must at some time have known better days, for this room, like Bredon's own, was generously proportioned, and could clearly be used as a bed-sitting-room. But the wall-paper had seen long service; the decorations were mean, the furniture shabby; it was not the sort of accommodation that would attract a rich man from Pullford, but for the reputation the place had for fishing and the want of any rival establishment. Chilthorpe, in spite of its possibilities of water-power, had no electric light; but the inn, with one or two neighbouring houses, was lighted by acetylene gas from a plant which served the Vicarage and the Parish Hall. These unpleasant fumes, still hanging in the air after two days, were responsible, it seemed, for the tragic loading of the bed which stood beside them.

To this last, Bredon paid little attention. He had no expert medical knowledge, and the cause of death was unquestioned; both the local man and a doctor whom the police had called in were positive that the symptoms were those of gas poisoning, and that no other symptoms were present; there were no marks of violence, no indications, even, of a struggle; the man had died, it seemed, in his sleep as if from an overdose of anaesthetic. Beside his bed stood a glass slightly encrusted with some whitish mixture; Bredon turned towards Leyland with an inquiring look as his eye met it.

'No good,' said Leyland. 'We had it analysed, and it's quite a mild sort of sleeping-draught. He sometimes took them, it seems, because he slept badly, especially in a strange bed. But there's no vice in the thing; it wouldn't kill a man, however heavily he doped himself with it, the doctor says.'

'Of course, it explains why he slept so soundly, and didn't notice the gas leaking.'

'It does that; and, if it comes to that, it sets me wondering a little. I mean, supposing it was murder, it looks as if it was done by somebody who knew Mottram's habits.'

'If it was murder, yes. But if it was suicide, it's easy to understand a man's doping himself, so that he should die off more painlessly. The only thing it doesn't look like is an accident, because it would be rather a coincidence that he should happen to be laid out by a sleeping-draught just on the very night when the gas was left on. I'd like to have a look at this gas.'

There was a bracket on the wall, not far from the door, which had been, originally, the only light in the room. But

for bed-sitting-room purposes a special fitting had been
added to this, giving a second vent for the gas; and this
new vent was connected, by a long piece of rubber tubing,
with a standard lamp that stood on the writing-table near
the window. There were thus three taps in all, and all of
them close together on the bracket. One opened the jet on
the bracket itself, one led to the rubber tubing and the
standard lamp. The third was the oldest and closest to the
wall; it served to cut off the supply of gas from both pas-
sages at once. This third, main tap was turned off now; of
the other two, the one on the bracket was closed, the one
which led to the standard stood open.

'Is this how the taps were when the body was first
found?' asked Bredon.

'Exactly. Of course, we've turned them on and off
since, to make certain that the jets were both in working
order – they were, both of them. And we tried the taps for
finger-prints – with powder, you know.'

'Any results?'

'Only on the main tap. We could just trace where it
had been turned on, with the thumb pressing on the right-
hand side. But there were no marks of fingers turning it
off.'

'That's damned queer.'

'Gloves?'

'Oh, of course, you think it was murder. Still, if it was
murder, it should have been the murderer who turned it
on *and* off. Why did he conceal his traces in one case and
not in the other?'

'Well, as a matter of fact, it was Mottram who turned
the gas on. At the main, that is. The tap of the standard
seems to have been on all the time – at least, there were no
marks on it. That's queer, too.'

'Yes, if he wanted it to be known that he committed
suicide. But if he didn't, you see, the whole business may
have been bluff.'

'I see – you want it to be suicide masquerading as accident. I want it to be murder masquerading as suicide.
Your difficulty, it seems to me, is explaining how the tap
came to be turned off.'

'And yours?'

26

'I won't conceal it. The door was locked, with the key on the inside.'

'How did anybody get in, then, to find the corpus?'

'Broke down the door. It was rotten, like everything else in this house, and the hinges pulled their screws out. You can see, there, where we've put fresh screws in since.'

'Door locked on the inside. And the window?' Bredon crossed to the other side of the room. 'Barred, eh?' It was an old-fashioned lattice window, with iron bars on the inside to protect it from unauthorized approach. The window itself opened outwards, its movements free until it reached an angle of forty-five degrees; at that point it passed over a spring catch which made it fast. It was so made fast now that Bredon examined it.

'This too?' he asked. 'Was the window just like this?'

'Just like that. Wide open, so that it's hard to see why the gas didn't blow out of doors almost as soon as it escaped – there was a high wind on Monday night, Brinkman tells me. And yet, with those bars, it seems impossible that anyone should have come in through it.'

'I think you're going to have difficulties over your murder theory.'

'So are you, Bredon, over your suicide theory. Look at that shirt over there; the studs carefully put in overnight; and it's a clean shirt, mark you; the outside buttonholes haven't been pierced. Do you mean to tell me that a man who is going to commit suicide is going to let himself in for all that tiresome process of putting studs in before he goes to bed?'

'And do you mean to tell me that a man goes out fishing in a boiled shirt?'

'Yes, if he's a successful manufacturer. The idea that one wears special clothes when one is going to take exercise is an upper class theory. I tell you, I've seen a farmer getting in the hay in a dickey, merely to show that he was a farmer, not a farm labourer.'

'Well, grant the point; why shouldn't a man who wants to commit suicide put studs in his shirt to make it look as if it wasn't suicide? Remember, it was a matter of half a million to his heirs. Is that too heavy a price for the bother of it?'

'I see you're convinced; it's no good arguing with you. Otherwise, I'd have pointed out that he wound up his watch.'

'One does. To a man of methodical habit, it's an effort to leave a watch unwound. Was he a smoker?'

'Brinkman says not. And there are no signs of it anywhere.'

'The law ought to compel people to smoke. In bed, especially – we should have got some very nice indications of what he was really up to if he had smoked in bed. But I see he wasn't a bedroom smoker in any case; here's a solitary match which has only been used to light the gas – he hasn't burnt a quarter of an inch of it.'

'That match worries me too. There's a box on the mantelpiece, but those are ordinary safeties. This is a smaller kind altogether, and I can't find any of them in his pockets.'

'The maid might have been in before him and lighted the gas.'

'They never do. At least, Mrs Davis says they never do.'

'It was dark when he went to bed?'

'About ten o'clock, Brinkman says. You would be able to see your way then, but not much more. And he must have lit the gas, to put the studs in his shirt – besides he's left some writing which was probably done late the night before last, though we can't prove it.'

'Writing! Anything important?'

'Only a letter to some local rag at Pullford. Here it is, if you want to read it.' And Leyland handed Bredon a letter from the blotting-pad on the table. It ran:

To the Editor of the *Pullford Examiner*

DEAR SIR,

Your correspondent, 'Brutus', in complaining of the closing of the Mottram Recreation Grounds at the hour of seven P.M., describes these grounds as having been 'presented to the town with money wrung from the pockets of the poor'. Now, Sir, I have nothing to do with the action of the Town Council in opening the Recreation Grounds or closing same. I write only as a private citizen who has done my best to make life amenable for the citizens of Pullford, to know why my name should be dragged into this controversy, and in the very injurious terms he has done. Such recreation grounds were presented by me twelve years ago to the townspeople of Pullford, not as 'blood-money' at all, but because I wanted them, and especially the kiddies, to get a breath of God's open air now and again. If 'Brutus' will be kind enough to supply chapter and verse, show-ing where or how operatives in my pay have received less pay than what they ought to have done –

At this point the letter closed abruptly.

'He wasn't very handy with his pen,' observed Bredon. 'I suppose friend Brinkman would have had to get on to this in the morning, and put it into English. Yes, I know what you're going to say; if the man had foreseen his end, he either wouldn't have taken the trouble to start the letter, or else he'd have taken the trouble to finish it. But I tell you, I don't like this letter. I say, we must be getting down to dinner; attract suspicion, what, if we're found nosing round up here too long? All right, Leyland, I won't spoil your sport. What about having a fiver on it – suicide or murder?'

'I don't mind if I do. What about telling one another how we get on?'

'Let's be quite free about that. But each side shall keep notes of the case from day to day, putting down his suspi-cions and his reasons for them, and we'll compare notes afterwards. Ah, is that Mrs Davis? All right, we're just coming.'

CHAPTER 5

Supper, and Mr Brinkman

MRS DAVIS's cuisine, if it did not quite justify all the ironic comments of the old gentleman, lent some colour to them. With the adjectival trick of her class, she always underestimated quantity, referring to a large tureen as 'a drop of soup', and overestimated quality, daily suggesting for her guests' supper 'a nice chop'. The chop always appeared; the nice chop (as the old gentleman pointed out) would have been a pleasant change. As surely as you had eggs and bacon for breakfast, so surely you had a chop for supper; 'and some nice fruit to follow' heralded the entrance of a depressed blancmange (which Mrs Davis called 'shape', after its principal attribute) and some cold greengages. These must have come from Alcinous's garden, for at no time of the year were they out of season. If Angela had stayed in the house for a fortnight, it is probable that she would have taken Mrs Davis in hand, and inspired her with larger ideas. As it was, she submitted, feeling that a suicide in the house was sufficiently unsettling for Mrs Davis without further upheavals.

The coffee-room at the 'Load of Mischief' was not large enough to let the company distribute itself at different tables, each party conversing in low tones and eyeing its neighbours with suspicion. A single long table accommodated them all, an arrangement which called for a constant exercise of forced geniality. Bredon and Leyland were both in a mood of contemplation, puzzling out the secret of the room upstairs; Brinkman was plainly nervous, and eager to avoid discussing the tragedy; Angela knew, from experience in such situations, the value of silence. Only the old gentleman seemed quite at his ease, dragging in the subject of Mottram with complete sangfroid, and in a tone of irony which seemed inseparable from his personality. Brinkman parried these topical references with considerable adroitness, showing himself as he did so a travelled man and a man of intelligence, though without much gift of humour.

Thus, in reply to a conventional question about his day's sport, the old gentleman returned, 'No, I cannot say that I caught any. I think, however, that I may claim, without boasting, to have frightened a few of them. It is an extraordinary thing to me that Mottram, who was one of your grotesquely rich men, should have come down for his fishing to an impossible place like this, where every rise deserves a paragraph in the local paper. If I were odiously rich, I would go to one of those places in Scotland, or Norway even, though I confess that I loathe the Scandinavians. I have never met them, but the extravagant praise bestowed upon them by my childhood's geography books makes them detestable to me.'

'I think,' said Brinkman, 'that you would find some redeeming vices among the Swedes. But poor Mottram's reason was a simple one: he belonged to these parts; Chilthorpe was his home town.'

'Indeed,' said the old gentleman, wincing slightly at the Americanism.

'Oo, yes,' said Angela, 'we saw Mottram on the map. Was he a sort of local squire, then?'

'Nothing of that sort,' replied Brinkman. 'His people took their name from the place, not the other way round. He started here with a big shop, which he turned over to some relations of his when he made good at Pullford. He quarrelled with them afterwards, but he always had a sentimental feeling for the place. It's astonishing what a number of group names there are still left in England. There is no clan system to explain it. Yet I suppose every tenth family in this place is called Pillock.'

'It suggests the accident of birth,' admitted the old gentleman, 'rather than choice. And poor Mottram's family, you say, came from the district?'

'They had been here, I believe, for generations. But this habit of naming the man from the place is curiously English. Most nations have the patronymic instinct; the Welsh, for example, or the Russians. But with us, apparently, if a stranger moved into a new district, he became John of Chilthorpe, and his descendants were Chilthorpes for ever.'

31

'A strange taste,' pursued the old gentleman, harping on the unwelcome subject, 'to want to come and lay your bones among your ancestors. It causes so much fuss and even scandal. For myself, if I ever decided to put a term to my own existence, I should go to some abominable place – Margate, for example – and try to give it a bad name by being washed up just underneath the pier.'

'You would fail, sir,' objected Brinkman; 'I mean, as far as giving it a bad name was concerned. You do not give things a good name or a bad name nowadays; you only give them an advertisement. I honestly believe that if a firm advertised its own cigarettes as beastly, it would draw money from an inquisitive public.'

'Mrs Davis has had an inquisitive public today. I assure you, when I went out this morning I was followed for a considerable distance by a crowd of small boys, who probably thought that I intended to drag the river. By the way, if they do drag the river, it will be interesting to find out whether there were, after all, any fish in it. You will let me be present, Sir?' – and he turned to Leyland, who was plainly annoyed by the appeal. Angela had to strike in, and ask who was the character in *Happy Thoughts* who was always asking his friend to come down and drag the pond. So the uneasy conversation zigzagged on, Mr Pulteney always returning to the subject which occupied their thoughts, the rest heading him off. Bredon was deliberately silent. He meant to have an interview with Brinkman afterwards, and he was determined that Brinkman should have no chance of sizing him up beforehand.

The opportunity was found without difficulty after supper; Brinkman succumbed at once to the offer of a cigar and a walk in the clear air of the summer evening. Bredon had suggested sitting on the bridge, but it was found that at that hour of the evening all the seating accommodation was already booked. Brinkman then proposed a visit to the Long Pool, but Bredon excused himself on the ground of distance. They climbed a little way up the hill-road, and found one of those benches, seldom occupied, which seem to issue their invitation to travellers who are short of breath. Here they could rest in solitude, watching cloud after cloud as it turned to purple in the dying sunlight, and the shadows gathering darker over the hill crests.

'I'm from the Indescribable, you know. Expect Mrs Davis has told you. I'd better show you my card-case so that you can see it's correct. They send me to fool round, you know, when this sort of thing happens. Have to be careful, I suppose.' ('This Brinkman,' he had said to Angela, 'must take me for a bit of a chump; if possible, worse than I am.')

'I don't quite see –' began Brinkman.

'Oh, the old thing, suicide, you know. Mark you, they don't absolutely bar it. I've known 'em pay up when a fellow was obviously potty. But their rules are against it. What I say is, if a man has the pluck to do himself in, he ought to get away with the stakes. Well, all this must be a great nuisance to you, Mr Brickman –'

'Brinkman.'

'Sorry, always was a fool about names. Well, what I mean is, it can't be very pleasant for you to have so many people nosing round; but it's got to be done somehow, and you seem to be the right man to come to. D'you think there was anything wrong in the upper storey?'

'The man was as sane as you or I. I never knew a man with such a level head.'

'Well, that's important. You don't mind if I scribble a note or two? I've got such a wretched memory. Then, here's another thing; was the old fellow worried about anything? His health, for example?'

There was an infinitesimal pause; just for that fraction of a second which is fatal, because it shows that a man is making up his mind what to say. Then Brinkman said, 'Oh, there can be no doubt of that. I thought he'd been and told your people about it. He went to a doctor in London, and was told that he'd only got two more years to live.'

'Meaning, I suppose –'

'He never told me. He was always a peculiar man about his health; he got worried even if he had a boil on his neck. No, I don't think he was a hypochondriac; he was a man who'd had no experience of ill-health, and the least thing scared him. When he told me about his interview with the

33

specialist, he seemed all broken up, and I hadn't the heart to question him about it. Besides, it wasn't my place. I expect you'll find that he never told anyone.'

'One could ask the medico, I suppose. But they're devilish close, ain't they, those fellows?'

'You've got to find out his name first. Mottram was very secret about it; if he wrote to make an appointment, the letter wasn't sent through me. It's a difficult job, circularizing Harley Street.'

'All the same, the doctor in Pullford might know. He probably recommended somebody.'

'What doctor in Pullford? I don't believe Mottram's been to a doctor any time these last five years. I was always asking him to, these last few months, because he told me he was worried about his health, though he never told me what the symptoms were. It's difficult to explain his secretiveness to anybody who didn't know him. But, look here, if you're inclined to think that his story about going to a specialist was all a lie, you're on the wrong tack.'

'You feel certain of that?'

'Absolutely certain. Look at his position. In two years' time, he was due to get a whacking annuity from your Company if he lived. He was prepared to drop his claim if the Company would pay back half his premiums. You've heard that, I expect? Well, where was the sense of that, unless he really thought he was going to die?'

'You can't think of any other reason for his wanting to do himself in? Just bored with life, don't you know, or what not?'

'Talk sense, Mr Bredon. You know as well as I do that all the suicides one hears of come from money troubles, or disappointment in love, or sheer melancholia. There was no question of money troubles; his lawyers will tell you that. He was not at the time of life when men fall badly in love, bachelors, anyhow; and his name was never coupled with a woman's. And as for melancholia, nobody who knew him could suspect him of it.'

'I see you're quite convinced that it was suicide. No question of accident, you think, or of dirty work at the cross-roads? These rich men have enemies, don't they?'

'In story-books. But I doubt if any living soul would

34

have laid hands on Mottram. As for accident, how would you connect it with all this yarn about the specialist? And why was the door of his room locked when he died? You can ask the servants at Pullford; they'll tell you that his room was never locked when he was at home; and the Boots here will tell you that he had orders to bring in shaving-water first thing.'

'Oh, his door was locked, was it? Fact is, I've heard very little about how the thing was discovered. I suppose you were one of the party when the body was found?'

'I was. I'm not likely to forget it. Not that I've any objection to suicide, mark you. I think it's a fine thing, very often; and the Christian condemnation of it merely echoes a private quarrel between St Augustine and some heretics of his day. But it breaks you up, rather, when you find a man you said "Good night" to the night before, lying there all gassed... However, you want to know the details. The Boots tried to get in with the shaving-water, and found the door locked; tried to look through the key-hole and couldn't; came round to me and told me about it. I was afraid something must be wrong, and I didn't quite like breaking down the door with only the Boots to help me. Then I looked out of the window, and saw the doctor here, a man called Ferrers, going down to take his morning bathe. The Boots went and fetched him, and he agreed the only thing was to break down the door. Well, that was easier than we thought. There was a beastly smell of gas about, of course, even in the passage. The doctor went up to the gas, you know, and found it turned off. I don't know how that happened; the tap's very loose, anyhow, and I fancy he may have turned it off himself without knowing it. Then he went to the bed, and it didn't take him a couple of minutes to find out that poor old Mottram was dead, and what he'd died of. The key was found on the inside of the door, turned so that the lock was fastened. Between you and me, I have a feeling that Leyland is wondering about that tap. But it's obvious that nobody got into the room, and dead men don't turn off taps. I can't piece it together except as suicide myself. I'm afraid your Company will be able to call me as a witness.'

'Well, of course, it's all jam to them. Not that they

mind coughing up much, but it's the principle of the thing, you see. They don't like to encourage suicide. By the way, can you tell me who the heirs were? What I mean is, I suppose a man doesn't insure his life and then take it unless he makes certain who comes in for the bullion?'

'The heirs, as I was saying at supper, are local people. Actually a nephew, I believe – I didn't want to say more at the time, because I think, between ourselves, that Mr Pulteney shows rather too much curiosity. But Mottram quarrelled with this young fellow for some reason – he owns the big shop here; and I'm pretty certain he won't be mentioned in the will.'

'Then you don't know who the lucky fellow is?'

'Charities, I suppose. Mottram never discussed it with me. But I imagine you could find out from the solicitors, because it's bound to be common property before long in any case.'

Bredon consulted, or affected to consult, a list of entries in his pocket-book. 'Well, that's awfully kind of you; I think that's all I wanted to ask. Must think me a beastly interfering sort of fellow. Oh, one other thing – is your room anywhere near the one Mr Mottram had? Would you have heard any sounds in the night, I mean, if there'd been anything going on in his room above the ordinary?'

'My room's exactly above, and my window must have been open. If there was any suspicion of murder, I should be quite prepared to give evidence that there was nothing in the nature of a violent struggle. You see, I sleep pretty light, and that night I didn't get to sleep till after twelve. It was seven o'clock in the morning when we found him, and the doctor seemed to think he'd been dead some hours. I heard nothing at all from downstairs.'

'Well, I'm tremendously obliged to you. Perhaps we'd better be wandering back, eh? You're unmarried, of course, so you don't have people fussing about you when you sit out of an evening.' In this happy vein of rather foolish good-fellowship Bredon conducted his fellow-guest back to the inn; and it is to be presumed that Brinkman did not feel he had spent the evening in the company of a Napoleonic brain.

CHAPTER 6

An Ear at the Keyhole

ON their return to the coffee-room they found Mr
Pulteney in sole possession. He was solemnly filling in a
crossword in a daily paper about three weeks old. Leyland had gone off to the bar parlour, intent on picking
up the gossip of the village. Bredon excused himself and
went upstairs, to find that Angela was not yet thinking
of bed, she had only got tired of the crossword. 'Well,' she
asked, 'and what do you make of Mr Brinkman?'

'I think he's a bit deep; I think he knows just a little
more about all this than he says. However, I let him talk,
and did my best to make him think I was a fool.'

'That's just what I've been doing with Mr Pulteney.
At least, I've been playing the *ingénue*. I thought I was
going to get him to call me "My dear young lady" – I love
that; he very nearly did once or twice.'

'Did you find him deep?'

'Not in that way. Miles, I forbid you to suspect Mr
Pulteney; he's my favourite man. He told me that suicide
generally followed, instead of preceding, the arrival of
young ladies. I giggled.'

'I wish he'd drown himself. He's one too many in this
darned place. And it's all confusing enough without him.'

'Want me to put in some Watson work?'

'If you aren't wanting to go to bed.' Watson work
meant that Angela tried to suggest new ideas to her
husband under a mask of carefully assumed stupidity.
'You see, I'm all for suicide. My instincts tell me that it's
suicide. I can smell it in the air.'

'I only smell acetylene. Why suicide particularly?'

'Well, there's the locked door. I've still got to see the
Boots and verify Brinkman's facts; but a door locked on
the inside, with barred windows, makes nonsense of Leyland's idea.'

'But a murderer might want to lock the door, so as to
give himself time to escape.'

37

'Exactly; but he'd lock it on the outside. On the other hand, a locked door looks like suicide, because, unless Brinkman is lying, Mottram didn't lock his door as a rule; and the Boots had orders to go into the room with shaving-water that morning.'

'Why the Boots? Why not the maid?'

'Angela, don't be so painfully modern. Maid-servants at country hotels don't. They leave some tepid water on the mat, make a gentle rustling noise at the door, and tip-toe away. No, I'm sure he locked the door for fear Brinkman should come in in the middle – or Pulteney, of course, might have come to the wrong door by mistake. He wanted to be left undisturbed.'

'But not necessarily in order to commit suicide.'

'You mean he might have fallen asleep over something else he was doing? Writing a letter, for example to the *Pullford Examiner?* But in that case he wouldn't have been in bed. You can't gas yourself by accident except in your sleep. Then there's another thing – the Bertillon-mark on the gas. Leyland is smart enough to know the difference between the mark you leave when you turn it on and the mark you leave when you turn it off. But he won't follow out his own conclusions. If Mottram had gone to bed in the ordinary way, as he must have in the event of foul play or accident, we should have seen where he turned it off as well as where he turned it on. The point is, Mottram didn't turn the light on at all. He went to bed in the half-darkness, took his sleeping-draught, and turned on the gas.'

'But, angel pet, how could he write a long letter to the Pullford paper in the half-darkness? And how did he read his shocker in the half-darkness? Let's be just to poor Mr Leyland, though he is in the Force.'

'I was coming to that. Meanwhile, I say he didn't light the gas. Because if you want to light the gas you have to do it in two places, and the match he used, the only match we found in the room, had hardly burned for a second.'

'Then why did he strike a match at all?'

'I'm coming to that, too. Finally, there's the question of the taps. A murderer would want to make certain of doing his work quickly, therefore he would make sure that the gas was pouring out of both jets, the one on the bracket on the wall, and the one on the standard-lamp by the window. The suicide, if he means to die in his sleep, isn't in a hurry to go off. On the contrary, he wants to make sure that his sleeping-draught takes effect before the gas-fumes become objectionable. So he turns on only one of the two jets, and that is the one further away from him. Isn't that all right?'

'You are ingenious, you know, Miles, occasionally. I'm always so afraid that one day you'll find *me* out. Now let's hear all about the things you were just coming to.'

'Well, you see, it isn't a simple case of suicide. Why should it be? People who have taken out a Euthanasia policy don't want Tom, Dick, and Harry to know – more particularly they don't want Miles Bredon to know – that they have committed suicide. They have the habit, as I know from experience, of trying to put up a little problem in detection for me, the brutes.'

'You shouldn't be angry with them, Miles. After all, if they didn't, the Indescribable might sack you, and where would Francis' new tam-o'-shanter come from?'

'Don't interrupt, woman. This is a case of suicide with complications, and dashed ingenious ones. In the first place, we noticed that entry in the visitor's book. That's an attempt to make it look as if he expected a long stay here, before he went to bed. Actually, through not studying the habits of the Wilkinsons, he overshot himself there – a little too ingenious. *We* know that when he did that he was simply trying to lead us up the garden; but we were too clever for him.'

'Let me merely mention the fact that it was I who spotted that entry. But pray proceed.'

'Then he did two quite irreconcilable things – he took a sleeping draught, and he asked to be called early. Now, a man who's on a holiday, and is afraid he won't sleep, doesn't make arrangements to be called early in the morning. *We* know that he took the sleeping-draught so as to die painlessly; and as for being called early in the morning, it was probably so as to give the impression that his death was quite unpremeditated. He took several other precautions for the same reason.'

'Such as?'

'He wound up his watch. Leyland noticed that, but he didn't notice that it was an eight-day watch. A methodical person winds up his eight-day watch on Sunday; once more, Mottram was a tiny bit too ingenious. Then, he put the studs out ready in his shirt. Very few people, when they're on holiday, take the trouble to do that. Mottram did, because he wanted us to think that he meant to get up the next morning in the ordinary way.'

'And the next article?'

'The window. A murderer, not taking any risks, would shut the window or see that it was shut, before he turned the gas on. A man going to bed in the ordinary way would either shut it completely, or else open it to its full extent, where the hasp catches, so that in either case it shouldn't bang during the night. Mottram left his window ajar, not enough open to let the gas escape much. But he knew that in the morning the door would have to be knocked in, and with that sudden rush of air the window would swing open. Which is exactly what happened.'

'I believe he wrote and told you about all this beforehand.'

'Silence, woman. He left a shocker by his bedside, to make us think that he went to bed at peace with all the world. In real life, if you take a dose, you don't read yourself to sleep as well. Besides, if he had been wanting to read in bed, he would have brought the standard lamp over to his bedside, so as to put it out last thing. Further, he had a letter ready written, or rather, half-written, which he left on the blotting-pad. But he hadn't written it there – he wrote it downstairs; I found the place where he had blotted it on the pad in the dining-room. Once more, a deliberate effort to suggest that he had gone to sleep peacefully, leaving a job half-finished. And then, of course, there was the match.'

'You mean, he'd only struck it to give the impression that he'd lit the gas, but didn't really light it? I'm getting the hang of the thing, aren't I? By the way, he couldn't have lit another match and thrown it out of the window?'

'Very unlikely. Only smokers, and tidy ones at that, throw matches out of the window. He either had one match left in his pocket, or borrowed one from Brinkman. But he didn't use it; suicides like the dark. There's one other tiny point – you see that?' He took up a large, cheap Bible which stood at the bedside of their own room. 'There's a Society which provides those, and, of course, there's one for each room. Mottram had taken his away from the bedside and put it in a drawer. It's funny how superstitious we men are, when all's said and done.'

'That's a tiny bit grooly, isn't it? Well, when are you going to dig the grave at the cross-roads, and borrow a stake from the local carpenter?'

'Well, you see, there's just that trifling difficulty about the tap being turned off. Leyland is right in saying that dead men don't do that sort of thing.'

'What's Brinky's explanation?'

'Mr Brinkman, to whom you were only introduced three hours ago, thinks the doctor turned it off accidentally. That's nonsense, of course. His idea was that the tap was very loose, but it wasn't, really – Leyland had it loosened on purpose, so as to be able to turn it without obliterating the finger-marks. If it hadn't been stiff, of course, there'd have been no marks left at all. So there's a three-pipe problem for you, my dear Mrs Hudson.'

Angela's forehead wrinkled becomingly. 'Two problems, my poor old Lestrade. How did the tap get turned off, and why does Brinky want us to think it got turned off accidental? I always like you to have plenty of theories, because it keeps your mind active; but with my well-known womanly intuition I should say it was a plain issue between the locked door, which means suicide, and the turned-off tap, which means murder. Did I hear you putting a fiver on it with Leyland?'

'You did. There's dashed little you don't hear.'

'Well, if you've got a fiver on it, of course it's got to be suicide. That's a good, wifely point of view, isn't it? I wish it were the other way round; I believe I could account for that door if I were put to it. But I won't; I swear I won't. I wonder how Leyland's getting on?'

'Well, he's worse off than we are, because he's got to get over the door trouble, and he's got to find a motive for the murder, *and* a criminal to convict of it. We score there; if it's suicide, there can be no two theories about the criminal! And·we know the motive – partly, anyhow. Mottram did it in order to make certain of that half-million for his legatees. And we shall soon know who they were. The only motive that worries me is Brinkman's; why he's so keen on its being suicide? Perhaps the will would make that clear, too ... I can't work it out at present.' He began to stride up and down the room. 'I'm perfectly certain about that door. It's impossible that it should be a spring lock, in an old-fashioned hotel like this.' He went up to the door of their room, and bent down to examine it. Then, with startling suddenness, he turned the handle and threw it open. 'Angela, come here ... You see that picture in the passage? There's no wind to make it swing like that, is there?'

'You mean you think somebody's been ...'

'Just as I bent down to the door, I could have sworn I heard foot-steps going softly away. It must have been somebody actually at the key-hole.'

'Why didn't you run out?'

'Well, it makes it so dashed awkward, to find somebody listening and catch them at it. In some ways, it's much better to know that somebody has been listening, and for them not to know whether you know or not. It's confoundedly awkward, all the same.'

'Idiotic of us not to have remembered that we were in a country pub, and that servants in country pubs still do listen at key-holes.'

'Servants? Well, ye–es. But Pulteney's room is only just round that corner.'

'Miles, I will not have you talking of poor old Edward like that.'

'Who told you his name was Edward?'

'It must be; you've only to look at him. Anyhow, he will always be Edward to me. But he simply couldn't listen at a key-hole. He would regard it as a somewhat unconventional proceeding' (this with a fair imitation of Mr Pulteney's voice). 'Besides, he can't *nearly* have finished that crossword yet. He's very stupid without me to help him; he will always put down Emu when there's a bird of three letters.'

'Well, anyhow, Brinkman's room is only up one flight of stairs. As you say, it may be the servants, or even Mrs Davis herself; but I'd like to feel sure of that. I wonder how much of what we said was overheard.'

'Well, Miles, dear, you ought to know. Don't you remember how you listened at the kitchen door in old Solomon's house, and thought you heard a man's voice, and found out afterwards it was only the loud speaker?'

'Good God, why does one marry? Look here, I'm just going to have a look-round for old Leyland, and warn him that there's dirty work at the cross-roads.'

'Yes, he must be careful not to soliloquize too much.'

'Don't be silly. It's time you went to bed; I won't be more than half-an-hour or so.'

'Not beyond closing-time, in other words? Gosh, what a man! Well, walk quietly, and don't wake Edward.'

Bredon found Leyland still in the bar-parlour, listening patiently to the interminable theorizings of the oldest inhabitant. 'That's how it was, you see. Tried to turn off the gars, and didn't turn it off proper, that's what he did. He didn't think to lay hands on himself, stands to reason he didn't. What for should he, and him so rich and all? Mark you, I've known Mottram when he wasn't no higher than that chair yonder, not so much he wasn't; and I know what I'm talking about. I've seen suicides put away too, I have; I recollect poor Johny Pillock up at the toll-house; went mad, he did, and hung himself off of a tree the same as if it might be from the ceiling yonder. Ah! There wasn't no gars in them days. Good night, Mr Warren, and pleasant dreams to you; you mind them stairs in your front-garden. Yes, powerful rich Mottram he was ...' and so on without cessation or remorse. It was nearly closing-time before Bredon managed to drag the policeman away, and warn him that there were others (it appeared) besides themselves who were interested in the secret of the upstairs room.

CHAPTER 7

From Leyland's Note-book

Now that I have put that fiver on with Bredon, I begin to doubt my own conclusions. That is the extraordinary effect of having a 'will to believe'. As long as you have no prejudices in the case, no brief to maintain, you can form a theory and feel that it is a mathematical certainty. Directly you have a reason for wanting to believe the thing true, that same theory begins to look as if it had all sorts of holes in it. Or rather, the whole theory seems fantastic – you have been basing too much on insufficient evidence. Yesterday, I was as certain that the case was one of murder as I am certain of my own existence. Today, I am developing scruples. Let me get it all down on paper, anyhow; and I shall be able to show my working to Bredon afterwards, however the case turns out.

There is one indication which is absolutely vital, absolutely essential; that is the turning off of the tap. That is the pin-point of truth upon which any theory must rest. I don't say it's easy to explain the action; but it is an action, and the action demands an agent. The fact that the gas was tampered with would convince me of foul play, even if there were no other direct indications. There are such indications.

In the first place, the window. If the window had stood all night as it was found in the morning, wide open and held by its clasp, there could have been no death. Pulteney tells me that there was a strong east wind blowing most of the night; and you can trust a fisherman to be accurate in these matters. The window, then, like the gas, had been deliberately arranged in an artificial position between Mottram's death and the arrival of the rescue party. If the death had been accidental, the window would have been shut and remained shut all night. You do not leave a window half open, with nothing to fix it, on a windy night. If it had been a case of suicide, it is equally clear that the window would have remained shut all night.

44

If you are proposing to gas yourself, you do not take risks of the window blowing open and leaving you half-asphyxiated. There is only one explanation of the open window, as there is of the gas-tap; and that explanation involves the interference of a person or persons unknown.

Another direct indication is the match found in the grate. Bredon's suggestion that this match was used by the maid earlier on in the evening is quite impossible; there was a box on the mantelpiece, which would be plainly visible in daylight, and it was not one of those matches that was used. It was a smaller match, of a painfully ordinary kind; Brinkman uses such matches, and Pulteney, and probably every smoker within miles round. Now, the match was not used to light the gas. It would have been necessary to light the gas in two places, and the match would have burned some little way down the stem, whereas this one was put out almost as soon as it was lit. It must have been used, I think, to light the gas in the passage outside, but of this I cannot be sure. It was thrown carelessly into the grate because, no doubt, the nocturnal visitor assumed as a matter of course, that others like it would already have been thrown into the grate. As a matter of fact Mottram must have thrown the match he lit the gas with out of the window: I have not found it.

From various indications, it is fairly clear that Mottram did not foresee his end. Chief among these is the order which he gave that he was to be woken early in the morning. This might, of course, be bluff; but if so it was a very heartless kind of bluff, for it involved the disturbing of the whole household with the tragic news in the small hours, instead of leaving it to transpire after breakfast. And this leads us on to another point, which Bredon appears to have overlooked. A man who wants to be woken up early in the morning does not take a sleeping draught over-night. It follows that *Mottram did not really take the sleeping-draught.* And that means that the glass containing it was deliberately put by his bed to act as a blind. The medical evidence is not positive as to whether he actually took the stuff or not. My conjecture is, then, that the man who came in during the night – twice during the night – put a glass with the remains of a sleeping-draught

45

by the bed in order to create the impression that Mottram had committed suicide.

When I struck upon this idea, it threw a flood of light on various other details of the case. We have to deal with a murder who is anxious to create the impression that the victim has died by his own hand. It was for this reason that he left a half-finished letter of Mottram's on the table – a letter which Mottram had actually written downstairs; this would look like the regular suicide's dodge of trying to cover up his tracks by leaving a half-finished document about. It would make a mind like Bredon's suspect suicide at once. The same may be said of the ridiculous care with which the dead man was supposed to have wound up an eight-day watch before retiring; it was a piece of bluff which in itself would deceive nobody; but here it was a double bluff, and I expect it has deceived Bredon. He will see everywhere the marks of a suicide covering up his tracks, which is exactly what the murderer meant him to see.

The thing begins to take shape in my mind, then, as follows. When he feels confident that his victim is asleep, the murderer tip-toes into the room, puts down the glass by the bed-side and the letter on the table; winds up the watch (a very silent one); and then goes over to the gas, wipes off with a rag the mark of Mottram's hand turning it off, and then, with the same rag, gently turns it on once more. The window is already shut. He tip-toes out of the door, and waits for an hour or two till the gas has done its deadly work. Then, for some reason, he returns; for what reason, I cannot at the present determine. Once he had taken all these precautions, it must have looked to him as if a verdict of suicide was a foregone conclusion. But it is a trick of the murderer – due, some think, to the workings of a guilty conscience – to revisit the scene of his crime and spoil the whole effect of it. It is this reason, of course, that I must find out before I am certain of my case; leaving aside all further questions as to the murderer's identity and his motives.

In fact, there are two problems, a problem of why and a problem of how. *Why* did the murderer turn the gas off? And *how* did he leave the door locked behind him? I suspect that the answer to the first question is, as I have said, merely psychological; it was some momentary instinct of bravado, or remorse, or sheer lunacy ... The answer to the second question must be something more complicated. In the abstract it is, I suppose, possible to turn a key in a lock from the wrong side, by using a piece of wire or some such instrument. But it is almost inconceivable that a man could do this without leaving scratches on the key; I have examined the key very carefully, and there are no scratches. Bredon, I can see, hopes to arrive at some different conclusion about the evidence; somebody, he thinks, is lying. But Brinkman, and Ferrers, the doctor, and the Boots, all rushed into the room at the same moment. Ferrers is an honest man, and I am sure he is telling the truth when he says he found the gas turned off; and he went to it at once, before either of the others had time to interfere. It was the Boots who found the key on the inside of the door, and the Boots will not do for the murderer; a man with one hand cannot have done conjuring tricks with a lock. Brinkman's own evidence is perfectly straightforward, and consistent with that of the others. He seems secretive, but that, I think, is the fellow's manner. I cannot at present see any motive which could have made him want to do away with Mottram; and the two seem to have been on intimate terms, and there is no evidence of a quarrel.

I am inclined to exonerate Pulteney of all knowledge, even of all interest in the affair. He was a complete stranger to Mottram, as far as I can discover. But suspicion may equally well fall on people outside the house; for, although the doors of the inn were locked, there is a practicable window on the ground floor, which is not always shut at night. Mottram was known in Chilthorpe and had lived there when he was young; there is the chance, then, of a local vendetta. Pullford is only twenty miles or so distant; and in Pullford he may easily have had enemies; the letter from 'Brutus' shows that. But, since the salient fact about Mottram was his wealth, it seems obvious that the first question to be settled is that of his testamentary dispositions. I must telegraph to London tomorrow for full information about these, and pursue my local inquiries in the meantime. The only person on the spot who has any close

47

tie of blood with the deceased is the young fellow who owns the big shop here. He is Mottram's nephew; Mottram himself started it long ago, and afterwards made it over to his sister and her husband, both of whom are now dead. Unfortunately for himself, the young man seems to have been something of a radical, and he made an injudicious speech at the time when Mottram was proposing to run himself as an Independent Parliamentary candidate for the constituency. There was a quarrel; and Mrs Davis thinks that the two never met again.

These are only my first impressions. They may have to be revised drastically as the case proceeds. But of one thing I am confident – there has been foul play, and the effort to represent it as a case of suicide is necessarily doomed to failure.

CHAPTER 8

The Bishop at Home

ANGELA and her husband breakfasted late next morning. Leyland came in as they were finishing, his manner full of excitement.

'Mrs Davis,' he explained, 'has been talking to me.'

'Don't be led on too much by that,' said Angela. 'It has happened to others.'

'No, but I mean Mrs Davis has been saying something.'

'That is far more unusual,' assented Bredon. 'Let's hear all about it. Angela ...'

'Mrs Bredon,' said Angela firmly, 'has been associated with me in many of my cases, and you may speak freely in her presence. Cough it up, Mr Leyland; nothing is going to separate me from this piece of toast.'

'Oh, there's nothing private about it particularly. But I thought perhaps you might help. You see, Mrs Davis says that Mottram was expecting a visitor to turn up in the morning and go out fishing with him.'

'A mysterious stranger?' suggested Angela. 'Carrying a blunt instrument?'

'Well, no, as a matter of fact it was the Bishop of Pullford. Do you know Pullford at all?'

'Nothing is hidden from us, Mr Leyland. They make drain-pipes there, not perambulators, as some have supposed. The parish church is a fine specimen of early Perp. It has been the seat of a R. Cath. Bishopric – oh, I suppose that's the man?'

'So Mrs Davis explained. A very genial man. Not one of your stand-offish ones. He was expected, it seems, by the first train, which gets in about ten. Mottram left word that he was to be called early, because he wanted to get at the fishing, and the Bishop, when he arrived, was to be asked to join Mr Mottram on the river; he would be at the Long Pool. He'd been down here before, apparently as Mottram's guest. Now, it's obvious that we had better find out what the Bishop has to say about all this. I'd go

49

myself, only for one thing I don't quite like leaving Chilthorpe while my suspicions' (he dropped his voice) 'are so undefined; and for another thing I'm telegraphing up to London for details about the will, and I want to be certain that the answer comes straight to my own hands. And the inquest is at four this afternoon; I can't risk being late for that. I was wondering whether you and Mrs Bredon would care to run over there? It would take you less than an hour in the car, and if you went as representing the Indescribable, it would make it all rather less – official. Then I thought perhaps at the end of the day we might swap information.'

'What about it, Angy?'

'I don't think I shall come and see the Bishop. It doesn't sound quite proper, somehow. But I'll drive you into Pullford, and sit at the hotel for a bit and have luncheon there, and you can pick me up.'

'All right. I say, though,' he added piteously, 'shall I have to go and change my suit?'

'Not for a moment. You can explain to the Bishop that your Sunday trousers are in pawn; if he's really genial he'll appreciate that. Besides, that tweed suit makes you look like a good-natured sort of ass; and that's what you want, isn't it? After all, if you do stay to lunch, it will only be a bachelor party.'

'Very well, then, we'll go. Just when I was beginning to like Chilthorpe. Look here, Leyland, you aren't expecting me to serve a summons on the bishop, or clap the darbies on him, or anything? Because if so you'd better go yourself.'

'Oh, no, I don't suspect the bishop – not particularly, that is. I just want to know what he can tell us about Mottram's movements immediately before his death, and what sort of man he was generally. He may even know something about the will; but there's no need to drag that topic in, because my telegram ought to produce full information about that. Thanks awfully. And we'll pool the day's information, eh?'

'Done. I say, though, I think I'd better just wire to the Bishop, to make sure that he's at home, and ready to receive a stray spy. Then we can start at elevenish.'

As Bredon returned from sending the telegram, he was waylaid, to his surprise, by Mr Pulteney, who was fooling about with rods and reels and things in the front hall. 'I wonder if I might make a suggestion to you, Mr Bredon,' he said. 'I despise myself for the weakness, but you know how it is. Every man thinks in his heart that he would have made a good detective. I ought to know better at my age, but the foul fiend keeps urging me to point something out to you.'

Bredon smiled at the elaborate address. 'I should like to hear it awfully,' he said. 'After all, detection is only a mixture of common sense and special knowledge; so why shouldn't we all put something into the pot?'

'It is special knowledge that is in question here; otherwise I would not have ventured to approach you. You see that rod? It is, as you doubtless know, Mottram's; it is the one which he intended to take out with him on that fatal morning. You see those flies on it?'

They looked to Bredon very much like any other flies, and he said so.

'Exactly. That is where special knowledge comes in. I don't know this river very well; but I do know that it would be ridiculous to try and fish this river with those particular flies, especially at this time of the year and after the weather we've been having. And I do know that a man like Mottram, who had been fishing this river year after year, couldn't possibly have imagined that it was any use taking those flies down to the Long Pool. I only mention it, because it makes me rather wonder whether Mottram really came down here to fish. Well, I must be starting for the river. Still nursing the unconquerable hope. Good morning.' And, with one of his sudden gestures, the old gentleman was gone.

A telegram came in admirably good time, assuring Bredon that the Bishop would be delighted to see him. It was little after eleven when the car took the road again; this time their way brought them closer to the Busk, and gave them a better view of its curious formation. A narrow gorge opened beneath them, and they looked down into deep pools overhung by smooth rocks that the water had eaten away at their base. There was no actual waterfall,

51

but the stream always hurried downwards, chuckling to itself under and around boulders which interrupted its course. 'I think Pulteney overestimates the danger of having his river dragged,' observed Bredon. 'You couldn't drag that part of it; and with all those shelves of rocks, a corpse might lie for days undiscovered, and no one the wiser. I'm glad that it's a death by gas, not by drowning.'

Their road now climbed on to the moors, and they began to draw closer to a desolate kind of civilization. Little factory towns which had sprung up when direct water-power was in demand, and continued a precarious existence, perched on those barren slopes, now that water-power had been displaced by steam, were the milestones of their route. They were jolted on a pavement of villainous sets; the air grew dim with smoke-haze, and the moorland blackened with their approach to the haunts of men. At last tram lines met them, announcing the outskirts of Pullford. 'I'm getting the needle rather about this interview,' confessed Bredon. 'What does one do by way of making oneself popular with a Catholic Bishop?' he demanded of Angela, who was convent-bred.

'Well, the right thing is to go down on one knee and kiss his ring. I don't think you'd make much of a show at it; we ought to have practised it before we left Chilthorpe. But I don't suppose he'll eat you.' Bredon tried to rearrange his ideas about Bishops. He remembered the ceremony of being confirmed at school; a long, tiresome service, with an interminable address, in which he and fifty of his compeers were adjured to play for their side. He remembered another bishop, met in a friend's rooms at Oxford; a hand laid on his shoulder, and an intolerably earnest voice asking whether he had ever thought of taking Holy Orders. Was that the sort of thing? Or was he rather to expect some silken-tongued courtier, in purple and fine linen, pledging him in rich liqueurs (as in the advertisements) and lying to him smoothly (as in the story-books)? Was he to be embarrassed by pietism, or to be hoodwinked by a practised intriguer? Anyhow, he would know the worst before long now. They drew up at the centre of the town before a vast, smoke-grimed hotel which promised every sort of discomfort; and Bredon, after asking his way to the Catholic Cathedral, and steadying himself with a vermouth, went out to face the interview.

The Cathedral house proved to be a good specimen of that curious municipal Gothic, which is the curse of all institutions founded in 1850. The kind of house which is characterized by the guide books as fine, by its immates as beastly. The large room into which Bredon was shown was at least equally cheerless. It was half-panelled in atrocious pitch-pine, and it had heavy, ecclesiastical-looking chairs which discouraged all attempts at repose. There was a gas stove in the fireplace. Previous occupants of the See of Pullford lined the walls, in the worst possible style of portraiture. A plaster Madonna, of the kind that is successively exiled from the church to the sacristy, and from the sacristy to the presbytery, at once caught and repelled the eye. In point of fact the room is never used, except by the canons of Pullford when they vest for the chapter Mass, and by the strange visitor who looks a little too important to be left in the waiting-room downstairs.

A door opened at the end of the room, and through it came a tall man dressed in black with a dash of red, whose welcome made you forget at once all the chill of the reception room. The face was strong and determined, yet unaffectedly benevolent; the eyes met you squarely, and did not languish at you; the manner was one of embarrassed dignity, with no suggestion of personal greatness. You did not feel that there was the slightest danger of being asked whether you meant to take orders. You did not catch the smallest hint of policy or of priestcraft. Bredon made a gesture as if to carry out Angela's uncomfortable prescription; but the hand that had caught his was at once withdrawn in obvious deprecation. He had come there as a spy, expecting to be spied upon; he found himself mysteriously fitting into this strange household as an old friend.

'I'm so sorry to have kept you waiting, Mr Brendan.' (The Chilthorpe post office is not at its best with proper names.) 'Come inside, please. So you've come to have a word about poor old Mottram? He was an old friend of ours here, you know, and a close neighbour. You had a

splendid morning for motoring. Come in, please.' And
Bredon found himself in a much smaller room, the obvious
sanctum of a bachelor. There were pipes about, and pipe-
cleaners; there was a pleasant litter of documents on the
table; there was a piano standing open, as pianos do when
people are accustomed to strum on them for mere pleasure;
there was a quite unashamed loud speaker in one corner.
The chair into which the visitor was shepherded was
voluminous and comfortable; you could not sit nervously
on the edge of it if you tried. Instinctively, in such a room,
your hand felt for your tobacco-pouch. Would Mr Brendan take anything before dinner? Dinner was due in
three-quarters of an hour. Yes, it was a very sad business
about poor Mottram. There was a feeling of genuine
regret in the town.

'I don't really know whether I'd any right to trespass
on my Lordship's – on your Lordship's time at all,' began
Bredon, fighting down a growing sense of familiarity. 'It
was only that the landlady told us this morning you were
expected to join Mottram at Chilthorpe just on the
morning when he died. So we naturally thought you
might have known something about his movements and
his plans. When I say "we", I mean that I'm more or less
working in with the police, because the inspector down
there happens to be a man I know.' (Dash it all, why was
he putting all his cards on the table like this?)

'Oh, of course, I should be only too glad if I can be of
any use. The papers have just mentioned the death as if it
were an accident, but one of my priests was telling me
there is a rumour in the town that the poor fellow took his
own life. Well, of course, I don't think that very probable.'

'He was quite cheerful, you mean, when you last saw
him?'

'Well, I wouldn't say cheerful, exactly; but, you see, he
was always a bit of a dismal Jimmy. But he was in here
one evening not a week ago, very glad to be going off for
his holiday, and full of fishing plans. It was then he asked
me to come down and join him just for the day. Well,
there was a tempting hole in my engagement book, and
there's a useful train in the morning to Chilthorpe; so I
promised I would. Then the Vicar-General rang me up

the last thing at night and told me about an important interview with some Education person which he'd arranged behind my back. So I gave it up – one has to do what one's told – and was meaning to telegraph to Mottram in the morning. And then this sad news came along before I had time to telegraph at all.'

'Oh, the news got here as early as that?'

'Yes, that secretary of his wired to me, Brinkman. It was kind of him to think of me, for I know the man very little. I forget the exact words he used, *Regret to say Mr Mottram died last night, useless your coming,* something of that sort.'

'Do you know if he meant to make any long stay at Chilthorpe?'

'Brinkman would be able to tell you better than I could; but I fancy they generally spent about a fortnight there every year. Mottram himself, I daresay you know, came from those parts. So far as I knew, this was to be the regular yearly visit. Honestly, I can't think why he should have been at pains to ask me down if there had been any idea of suicide in his mind. Of course, if there was definite insanity, that's a different thing. But there was nothing about him to suggest it.'

'Do I understand that Mottram belonged to your – that Mottram was a Catholic?'

'Oh, dear no. I don't think he was a church-goer at all. I think he believed in Almighty God, you know; he was quite an intelligent man, though he had not had much schooling when he was young. But his friendship with us was just a matter of chance – that and the fact that his house is so close to us. He was always very kindly disposed towards us – a peculiar man, Mr Brendan, and a very obstinate man in some ways. He liked being in the right, and proving himself in the right; but he was broad-minded in religious matters, very.'

'You don't think that he would have shrunk from the idea of suicide – on any moral grounds, I mean?'

'He did defend suicide in a chat we had the other day. Of course, my own feeling is that by the time a man has got to the state of nerves in which suicide seems the only way out, he has generally got beyond the stage at which he can really sit down and argue whether it is right or wrong. At least, one hopes so. I don't think that a person who defends suicide in the abstract is any more the likely to commit suicide for that, or vice versa. Apart from grace, of course. But it's the absence of motive, Mr Brendan. Why should Mottram have wanted to take his own life?'

'Well, my Lord, I'm afraid I see these things from an uncharitable angle. You see, my business is all connected with insurance; and Mottram was insured with us, and insured heavily.'

'Well, there you are, you see; you have the experience and I haven't. But doesn't it seem to you strange that a man in good health, who digests his meals, and has no worries, should take his own life in the hope of benefiting his heirs, whoever they may prove to be? He had no family, you must remember.'

'In good health? Then ... then he didn't mention anything to you about his life prospects?'

'I can't say that he did; but he always seemed to enjoy good health. Why, was there anything wrong?'

'My Lord, I think this ought to be confidential, if you don't mind. But, since you knew him so well, I think it's only fair to mention to you that Mottram had misgivings about his health.' And he narrated the story of Mottram's singular interview at the Indescribable Office. The Bishop looked grave when he had finished.

'Dear, dear, I'd no notion of that; no notion at all. And it's not clear even now what was wrong with him? Well, of course, that alters things. It must be a grave temptation for people who are suffering from a malignant disease, especially if it's a painful one; pain clouds the reason so, doesn't it? I wish I'd realized that he was in trouble, though it's very little one can do. But that's just like him; he was always a bit of a Stoic; fine, in a rugged sort of way; *it never did any good meeting troubles half-way*, he used to say to me. Well, money can't do everything for us.'

'He was enormously rich, I suppose?'

'Hardly that. He was very comfortably off, though. There will be a windfall, I suppose, coming to somebody.'

'He never mentioned to you, I suppose, what he meant to do with his money?'

'Well, of course, he used to say half-jokingly that he was going to provide for us; but I don't think he meant us to take that seriously. He had a kind of hankering after religion, you see, but he didn't get on well with religious people as a general thing. The Anglicans, he said, were all at sixes and sevens, and he couldn't bear a Church which didn't know its own mind. The Nonconformists, he said, did no sort of good in the town; all those fine chapels, and only thirty or forty people in each of them on a Sunday morning. He was a little unjust, I think, to the Nonconformists; they do a great deal of good, some of them. And about the Salvation Army he was extraordinarily bitter. So he used to say he'd sooner his money went to us than to any of the others. But I think that was only an ironic way he had with him; people who have made a lot of money are often fond of talking about what they're going to do with it. Of course, it would have made a lot of difference to us; but I don't think he meant to be taken seriously.'

'Well, I'm very much obliged to your Lordship; I think, perhaps, I ought to be ...'

'What, going away, and dinner on the table? No, no, Mr Brendan, that isn't how we treat our guests at Pullford. Just you come along, now, and be introduced to some of the reverend clergy. I know the "Load of Mischief", and those chops! Come on, and we'll send you off in better trim than you came.' It was evident that there was no help for it; Angela must wait.

57

CHAPTER 9

The Late Rector of Hipley

THE dinner-table left a blurred impression on Bredon, for all his habit of observing his fellow-men and analysing his feelings about them. The setting-out of the meal had faults that Angela would have condemned, and would have put right in no time; you were conscious at once that the household belonged to bachelors. Yet the meal itself and the cooking of it were of excellent quality; and it was thrown at you with a clamorous, insistent hospitality that made you feel like a guest of honour. The room seemed to be full of priests – there were five, perhaps, in reality, besides the Bishop – and every detail of their behaviour proved that they were free from any sense of formality or restraint; yet constant little attentions showed the guest that he was never forgotten. The topic of conversation which Bredon could recall most distinctly afterwards was a learned and almost technical discussion between the Bishop and the youngest priest present on the prospects of the local Soccer team for next year. Nothing fitted in, somehow, with his scheme of probabilities; there was a Father O'Shaughnessy, who had been born and bred in Pullford and never seemed to have been outside it; there was a Father Edwards, who talked with a violent Irish brogue. A teetotaller opposite kept plying him with Barsac.

It was perhaps a delicate attention that Bredon's next-door neighbour, on the side away from the Bishop, was the only other layman present. He was introduced as the Bishop's secretary; and he was the only man in the room who looked like a clergyman. He seemed some fifty years old; he was silent by habit, and spoke with a dry humour that seemed to amuse everybody except himself. Bredon could not help wondering how such a man came to occupy such a position at his time of life; for his voice betrayed University education, and he was plainly competent; yet he obviously thought of himself as a supernumerary in the

household. The riddle was solved when Bredon, in answer
to some question about his journey down to Chilthorpe,
explained that he did not come from London itself, but
from a village in Surrey, a place called Burrington.
'What,' said Mr Eames, the secretary, 'not Burrington
near Hipley?' And, when Bredon asked if he knew Hipley,
'Know it? I ought to. I was rector there for ten years.'

The picture of the rectory at Hipley stood out before
Bredon's mind; you see it from the main road. There is an
old-fashioned tennis-lawn in front of it; roses cluster round
it endearingly; there is a cool dignity about the Queen
Anne house, the terraces are spotlessly mowed. Yes, you
could put this man in clerical clothes, and he would fit
beautifully into that spacious garden; you saw him with
surplice fluttering in the breeze, going up the churchyard
path to ring the bell for evening service; that was his
atmosphere. And here, unfrocked by his own conscience,
he was living as a hired servant, almost a pensioner, in
this gaunt house, these cheerless rooms. ... You wondered
less at his silent habit, and his melancholy airs of speech.

Nothing creates intimacy like a common background
discovered among strangers. They belonged, it seemed, to
the same University, the same College; their periods were
widely different, but dons and scouts, the milestones of
short-lived undergraduate memory, were recalled, and
their mannerisms discussed; and when at the end of the
meal the Bishop rose, profuse in his apologies, to attend
a meeting, Eames volunteered to walk Bredon back to his
hotel. 'I thought there'd be no harm, my Lord, if we just
took a look in at poor Mottram's house; I daresay it
would interest Mr Bredon to see it. The house-keeper,' he
explained to Bredon 'is one of our people.'

The Bishop approved the suggestion; and with a chorus
of farewells they left the Cathedral House together.
'Well,' said Bredon, to his companion, 'you've got a
wonderful Bishop here.'

'Yes,' said Eames, 'the mind dwells with pleasure on
the thought of him. There are few of us for whom more
can be said than that.'

'I can't fit Mottram, from what I've heard of him, into
that household.'

'Because you're not a provincial. Our common roots are in Oxford and in London. But in a place like this people know one another because they are neighbours.'

'Even the clergy?'

'The Catholic clergy, anyhow. You see, our priests don't swap about from one diocese to another; they are tied to the soil. Consequently they are local men, most of them, and a local man feels at home with them.'

'Still ... for a man who had no religion particularly ... isn't it rather a challenge, to be up against your faith like that? I should have thought a man was bound to react one way or the other.'

'Not necessarily. It's astonishing what a lot of theoretical interest a man can take in the faith, and yet be miles away from it practically. Why, Mottram himself, about three weeks ago, was pestering us all about the old question of "the end justifying the means". Being a Protestant, of course he meant by that doing evil in order that good may come. He worried the life out of the Bishop, urging the most plausible reasons for maintaining that it was perfectly right. He simply couldn't see why the Bishop insisted you weren't ever allowed to do what's wrong, whatever comes of it. And the odd thing was, he really seemed to think he was being more Catholic over it than we were. However, all that bores you.'

'No, indeed. I want to know everything about Mottram; and it's silly to pretend that a man's religion doesn't matter. Was he thinking at all, do you suppose, of becoming a Catholic?'

Eames shrugged his shoulders. 'How can I tell? I don't think he really showed any disposition. But of course, he was a religious man in a way, he wasn't one of your Nogoddites, like Brinkman. You've met Brinkman?'

'Yes, I'm staying in the same hotel, you see. And I confess I'm interested in him, too. What do you make of him? Who is he, or where did Mottram pick him up?'

'I don't know. I don't like the little man. I don't even know what his nationality is; he's spent a long time in Paris, and I'm pretty sure he's not British. And mind you, he hated us. I think he had corresponded for some paper out in Paris; anyhow, he knew all the seedy anti-clericals;

and I rather think he was asked to leave. Mottram seems to have taken him on on the recommendation of a friend; he had some idea, I think, of doing a history of the town; and, of course, Brinkman can write. But Brinkman very seldom came in here, and when he did, he was like a dog among snakes. I daresay he thought the house was full of oubliettes. He'd got all that Continental anti-clericalism, you see. Here's the house.'

They turned up a short drive which led them through a heavily-walled park to the front door of a painfully middle-Victorian mansion. A mansion it must be called; it did not look like a house. Strange reminiscences of various styles, Gothic, Byzantine, Oriental, seemed to have been laid on by some external process to a red-brick abomination of the early seventies. Cream-coloured and slate-coloured tiles wove irrelevant patterns across the bare spaces of wall. Conservatories masked a good half of the lowest storey. It was exactly suited to be what it afterwards became, a kind of municipal museum, in which the historic antiquities of Pullford, such as they were, could be visited by the public on dreary Sunday afternoons.

'Now,' said Eames, 'does that give you Mottram's atmosphere?'

'God forbid,' replied Bredon.

'See then the penalty of too great riches. Only one man in a thousand can express his personality in his surroundings if he has a million of money to do it with. It wasn't Mottram, of course, who did this; but he would have built the same sort of horror if he hadn't taken it over from a predecessor like himself. And the rooms are as bad as the house.'

Eames was fully justified in this last criticism. The house was full of expensive bad taste; the crude work of local artists hung on the walls; bulging goddesses supported unnecessary capitals; velvet, and tarnished gilding, and multi-coloured slabs of marble completed the resemblance to a large station restaurant. Mottram had possessed no private household gods, had preserved no cherished knick-knacks. The house was the fruit of his money, not of his personality. He had given the architect a free hand, and in the midst of all that barbaric splendour he had lived, a homeless exile.

61

The housekeeper had little to add to what Bredon already knew. Her master usually went away for a holiday about that time in the year, and Mr Brinkman always went with him. He had expected to be away for a fortnight, or perhaps three weeks. He had not shown, to the servants at any rate, any signs of depression or anxiety; he had not left any parting messages to suggest a long absence. His letters were to be re-directed, as usual, to the 'Load of Mischief'. There had been none, as a matter of fact, except a few bills and circulars. She didn't think that Mr Mottram went to any of the Pullford doctors, regularly at least; and she had had no knowledge of his seeing the specialist in London. She did not remember Mr Mottram being ill, except for an occasional cold, though he did now and again take a sleeping-draught.

'It's quite true,' said Eames as they left the house, 'that we never noticed any signs of depression or anxiety in Mottram. But I do remember, only a short time ago, his seeming rather excited one evening when he was round with us. Or am I imagining it? Memory and imagination are such close neighbours. But I do think that when he asked the Bishop to go and stay down at Chilthorpe he seemed unnaturally insistent about it. He was fond of the Bishop, of course, but I shouldn't have thought he was as fond of him as all that. To hear him talk, you would think that it was going to make all the difference to him whether the Bishop shared his holiday or not.'

'Yes ... I wonder what that points to?'

'Anything or nothing. It's possible, of course, that he was feeling depressed, as he well might be; and thought that he wanted more than Brinkman's company to help him over a bad time. Or ... I don't know. He was always secretive. He gave the Bishop a car, you know; and took endless pains to find out beforehand what sort of car would be useful to him, without ever giving away what he was doing till the last moment. And the other evening – well, I feel now as if I'd felt then that he had something up his sleeve. But did I really feel it then? I don't know.'

'On the whole, though, you incline to the suicide theory?'

'I didn't say that. It's possible, isn't it, that a man who

had some premonition of a violent end might want company when he went to a lonely place like Chilthorpe?'

'Had he any enemies, do you think, in Pullford?'

'Who hasn't? But not that sort of enemies. He used, I fancy, to be something of a martinet with his workpeople, in the old manner. In America, a disgruntled employé sometimes satisfies his vendetta with a shot-gun. But in England we have no murdering classes. Even the burglars, I am told, make a principle of going unarmed, for fear they might be tempted to shoot. You would probably find two or three hundred men in Pullford who would grouse at Mottram's success and call him a blood-sucker, but not one who would up with a piece of lead-piping if he met him in a lonely lane.'

'I say, it's been very kind of you looking after me like this. I wish, if you've any time to spare in the next day or two, you would drop down to Chilthorpe and help me to make the case out. Or is that asking too much?'

'Not the least. The Bishop goes off to a Confirmation tomorrow, and I shall probably have time on my hands. If you think I could be of any use, I'll certainly look in. I like Chilthorpe; every prospect pleases and only chops are vile. No, I won't come in, thanks; I ought to be getting back now.'

Angela was a little inclined to be satirical at her husband's prolonged absence; but she seemed to have killed the time with some success. She had not even been reduced to going round the early Perp. Church. They made short work of the way back to Chilthorpe, and found Leyland eagerly awaiting them at the door of the hotel.

'Well,' he asked, 'have you found out anything about Mottram?'

'Not much, and that's a fact. Except that a man who strikes me as a competent observer thought he had noticed a certain amount of excitement in Mottram's manner last week, as if he had been more than ordinarily anxious to get the Bishop to stay with him. That, and the impression, made on the same observer, that he was keeping dark about something, had something up his sleeve. I have seen the house; it is a beastly place; and it has electric light laid on, of course. I have seen the housekeeper, an entirely harmless woman, partly Irish by extraction, who has nothing to add to what we know, and does not believe that Mottram habitually employed any of the Pullford doctors.'

'Well, and what about the Bishop?'

'Exactly, what about him? I find his atmosphere very difficult to convey. He was very nice to me, and very hospitable; he has not the overpowering manners of a great man, and yet his dignities seem to sit on him quite easily. He is entirely natural, and I am prepared to go bail for his being an honest man.'

'That,' said Leyland, 'is just as well.'

'How do you mean? Have you had the answer to your telegram?'

'I have, and a very full answer it is. The solicitors gave all the facts without a murmur. About fifteen years ago Mottram made a will which was chiefly in favour of his nephew. A few years later, he cancelled that will absolutely, and made another will, in which he devised his property to certain public purposes – stinkingly useless ones, as is the way of these very rich men. I can't remember it all; but he wants his house to be turned into a silly sort of museum, and he provides for the erection of a municipal art gallery – that sort of thing. But this is the important point. His Euthanasia policy was not mentioned at all in the later will. Three weeks ago he put in a codicil directing how the money he expects from the Indescribable is to be disposed of.'

'Namely, how?'

'The entire half-million goes to the Bishop of Pullford, to be administered by him for the benefit of his diocese, as he and his successors shall think fit.'

CHAPTER 10

The Bet Doubled

THERE was no time to discuss the implications of this unexpected announcement, for the inquest was just beginning, and neither Leyland nor Bredon could afford to miss
it. There was a decayed outbuilding which adjoined the
'Load of Mischief', the scene, you fancied, of the farmers'
ordinary in more prosperous times. Here the good men
and true were to deliver their verdict, and the coroner his
platitudes.

Brinkman's evidence need not be repeated here, for it
followed exactly the lines we already know. The local
doctor and the Boots corroborated his account so far as the
discovery of the corpse was concerned. Particular attention was naturally called to the tap and to the locked door.
The doctor was absolutely positive that the tap was turned
off when he reached it; the fumes had blown away a good
deal by that time, and his first action was to put a match
to both jets in turn. Neither gave the least promise of a
flame, although the jet on the standard stood open; there
was no doubt, then, that the main tap sufficiently con-
trolled both outlets. Asked whether he turned the main tap
on to experiment, the doctor said 'No', and was con-
gratulated by the coroner on his circumspection. The
work of the police would be much facilitated, observed
that prudent functionary, if people would leave things as
they found them. After testing the gas the doctor's next
action had been to attend to the patient. Much medical
detail followed at this point, but with no results that
would be new to us. Asked how long it would have taken
for the gas to cause asphyxiation, the doctor was uncertain. It all depended, he said, on the position of the
window, which must clearly at some time have blown
further open than it had been originally. It was his impression that the death must have occurred about one
o'clock in the morning; but there were no sure tests by

which the exact moment of death could be determined.

The Boots, by his own account, entered the room immediately after the doctor. The door of the room had fallen almost flat when it fell in; not quite flat, for it was not entirely separated from the lower hinge. The Boots made his way over this, and helped the doctor by supplying him with a match. When the doctor went across to the bed, he himself went to the window to throw the match out. Dr Ferrers had joined Mr Brinkman at the bed, so he devoted himself to examining, and trying to hoist up, the wreckage of the door. The lock was right out, and the key duly turned on the inside of the door. It was not usual for him to call guests in the morning, but he had arranged to do so on that particular occasion. He noticed the smell of gas even outside the door, but did not feel sure there was anything wrong until he tried the door and found it locked. It was not usual for guests to lock their doors in that hotel, although keys were provided for the purpose ... Yes, he did bend down and look through the keyhole, but it was completely dark – naturally, since the key was in the lock. He went and asked Mr Brinkman what he should do, because he was anxious not to go beyond his orders.

The barmaid had really nothing to contribute. She had not been into the room at all after six o'clock, or it might be half past on the Monday evening, when she went in to put everything to rights. Pressed to interpret this phrase, she said it meant turning down the corner of the bedclothes. She had not struck a match, naturally, since it was broad daylight. She had never noticed any leak of gas in that room since the plumber had paid a visit in the previous March. There was nothing wrong, she thought, about the catch of the window; certainly no visitor had ever complained of its fetching loose in the night. The Bible, she thought, had been by the bedside when she went into the room at six or it might have been half past. She did not move it, nor did she interfere in any way with the arrangements of the room.

Mrs Davis confirmed this evidence as far as it needed confirmation. It was she who had taken the order from Mottram about his being called early in the morning. He had spoken to her quite naturally, and said good night to her cheerfully.

Mr Pulteney's evidence was entirely negligible. He had noticed nothing the evening before, had heard nothing in the night, had not entered the room since the tragedy occurred.

The Coroner spread himself in his allocution to the jury. He reminded them that an escape of gas could not properly be described as an act of God. He pointed out that it was impossible to return a verdict of death from unknown causes, since the cause of death was known. If they were prepared to give any new explanation of the fact that the gas was turned off, they might bring in a verdict of death by misadventure, or by suicide; in the latter case, it was possible to add a rider saying that the deceased was of unsound mind. If they were prepared to give any new explanation of the locked door, it was possible for them to bring in a verdict of wilful murder against a person or persons unknown. In fact, the reader will see that the coroner was a man like himself.

The jury, unequal to the intellectual strain which seemed to be demanded of them, returned an open verdict. The coroner thanked them, and made them a little speech which had not really much bearing on the situation. He pointed out the superiority of electric light over gas; in a house lit by electric light this could never have happened. He called attention to the importance of making certain that the gas was turned off before you got into bed, and the almost equal importance of seeing that your window was well and truly opened. And so the inquest ended, and Mottram, who had expressed no desires in his will as to where or how he should be buried, was laid to rest next day in the churchyard of the little town which had seen his early struggles, and Pullford remembered him no more.

As soon as the inquest was over, Leyland and Bredon met, by arrangement, to discuss further the bearings of the new discovery. They avoided the inn itself, partly because the day's events had left it overcrowded, partly because they were afraid, since Bredon's experience the night before, of speaking to a concealed audience. A slight rain was falling, and they betook themselves to the back of the inn, where a rambling path led along the river bank through the ruins of an old mill. Next the disused mill-wheel there was a little room or shed, whose gaping walls and roof afforded, nevertheless, sufficient shelter from the weather. A 'rustic seat', made of knobby branches over-laid with dark brown varnish, offered uncomfortable repose. Draughts at the back of your neck, or sudden leakage in the slates above you, would cause you now and again to shift your attitude uneasily; but, since the 'Load of Mischief' did not abound with amenities in any case, they were content with their quarters.

'I confess I'm a little shaken,' admitted Bredon. 'Not that I see any logical reason for altering my own point of view; but I don't *want* it to be suicide now as much as I did. The Bishop is such a jolly old man; and he could so obviously do with half a million, if only to put in new wallpapers. ... He might even give his secretary a rise. I tell you, I hate the idea of advising the Company not to pay up. It can afford the money so easily. But I suppose I must have a sort of conscience about me somewhere; for I'm still determined to get at the truth. This codicil, you say, was put in less than three weeks ago?'

'Just about that. As nearly as I can calculate, it must have been just before, not after, Mottram's visit to the Indescribable.'

'The thing becomes more confusing than ever. If he did want to endow the diocese of Pullford, why did he offer to resign his Euthanasia claim on condition that we repaid half his premiums? And if he didn't want to endow the diocese of Pullford, why did he take the trouble of altering his will in its favour?'

'Remember, when he drew up the codicil he may not have seen the specialist.'

'That's true, too. ... Now, look here, supposing he hadn't put the codicil in, what would have become of the Euthanasia money? Would it have gone, like the rest, into these silly schemes of his about Art galleries?'

'No, it wasn't just a vague will, nothing about "all I die possessed of". The whole thing was itemized very clearly, and no allowance had been made at all for the disposal of the Euthanasia money. Consequently, if he hadn't made the codicil, the Euthanasia money would have gone to his next of kin.'

'In fact, to this nephew? Really, I begin to want to see this nephew.'

'You have seen him.'

'Seen him – where?'

'At the inquest. Didn't you notice a rather seedy little fellow, with a face like a rat, who was standing about in the porch just when it was over? That's your man; Simmonds his name is, and if you want to get a taste of his quality, nothing's easier, for he serves in his own shop. On a plea of braces trouble, shortage of cough lozenges, or what you will, his time is yours from ten in the morning to seven at night.'

'Yes, I noticed the little man. I can't say I was favourably prepossessed. But I must certainly improve the acquaintance. I suppose it's not fair to ask what you make of him?'

'Oh, personally I can't say I've made much of him. I had a talk, and his manner and statements seemed to be perfectly straightforward. No nervousness, no embarrassment.'

'There's one other thing about Mottram's will that's clearly important. You got it, I gather, from the solicitors; did you find out from them whether the terms of it were made public in any way?'

· 'About the main will they thought there was no secret. Mottram seems to have talked it over with members of the Pullford Town Council. Also, the lawyers were directed to send a full statement of it to young Simmonds, as a kind of rebuke; Simmonds, you see, had annoyed Mottram at the time. But this codicil was a different affair; it was extremely confidential.· Brinkman himself – though of course he may have been lying, or being discreet – professed ignorance of it. I should think it very improbable that anybody knows about it yet, except you and me and Mrs Bredon, and of course the lawyers themselves.'

'Then there's a chance, I suppose, that Simmonds thought, and still thinks, he is coming in for a windfall from our Company? Or do you think he didn't know Mottram was insured?'

'He must have; because the Euthanasia policy was explicitly mentioned in the earlier will, the one which was cancelled. So you are not the only person who's interested in young Simmonds. Well, what do you make of it all?'

'Let me tell you one thing; it wouldn't be fair if I didn't. About three weeks ago Mottram had an argument with the Bishop of Pullford on a matter of theology. Mottram was trying to persuade the Bishop that you were morally justified in doing evil in order that good might come of it.'

'I'm very much obliged for the information, old man, but I'm not much interested in these speculative questions. I'm concerned to hunt out the people who do evil, whether good comes of it or not.'

'But the information doesn't impress you?'

'Not much.'

'Very well, then. Will you double that bet?'

'Double the bet? You're mad! Why, I was just going to make the same offer, feeling sure you'd refuse. It's taking your money.'

'Never mind that. Are you on?'

'On? Why, I'm prepared to redouble if you like.'

'Done! That's twenty pounds. Now, would you like to hear my reading of the story?'

'By all means. And then I shall have the pleasure of putting you wise.'

'Well, from the first, the whole thing smelt of suicide to me. Every step Mottram took seemed to be the calculated step of a man who was leading up to some deliberate *dénouement*. He was mysterious, he was excited, when he went round the other night to the Cathedral House. When he came here, he made the most obvious attempts to try and behave as if everything was going on just as usual. He made fussy arrangements about being called in the morning; he pretended to have left a letter half-finished; he put a novel down by the bedside, wound up his watch, put studs in his shirt – he did everything to create the surface impression, good enough (he thought) for the coroner, that whatever else was the truth, suicide was out of the question. He made one or two slips there – writing down his name in the Visitors' book with a blank for his date of departure, as if any guest ever did that; putting

the flies ready on his rod, but (so Pulteney tells me) the
wrong kind of flies. To make sure that there was not a
verdict of suicide, he even made arrangements – through
Brinkman, through Mrs Davis, I don't know how – to
have the gas in his bedroom turned off again after it had
done its work. Then he tossed off his sleeping-draught,
turned the gas on, and got into bed. I was sure of all that,
even before I went over to Pullford, before you got the
telegram from London. What I couldn't understand was
the motive; and now that's as plain as daylight. He was
determined to endow the Pullford diocese with half a
million, so as to be sure of having his nest well lined in the
next world. He knew that Christian morality doesn't
permit suicide, but he thought he was all right, because
he was only doing evil in order that good might come of
it. And so he got rid of the spectre of a painful death from
disease, and at the same time made sure, he thought, of a
welcome on the other side, if there should prove to be an
eternity.'

'Well, that's your idea. I don't deny it hangs together.
But it comes up against two things – fatally, I think. If
Mottram was so set upon endowing the Pullford diocese,
why did he bequeath most of his fortune to a footling
Town Council, and only leave the diocese the one bit of
money which, if a verdict of suicide was given, could
never be touched? And granted that he was at pains to
get someone to turn off the gas for him, so as to avoid the
appearance of suicide, why did he tell that person to lock
the door, and leave the key on the wrong side? That's the
problem you've set yourself.'

'Oh, God knows, I don't see my way clear yet. But
there's the outlines of the thing. Now let's hear the *proxime
accessit* solution.'

'I feel inclined to apologize. I feel ashamed of being so
right. But you've asked for it. Look here, the thing which
has complicated this case so badly is the appearance of
bluff. At one moment it looked like suicide pretending to
be accident or murder; at another time it looked like
murder pretending to be suicide. But the great mountain-
ous fact that stands out is the turning off of the gas. In the
event of suicide, that was impossible; in the event of

71

murder, it was curiously needless. For it entirely removed the possibility of a suicide verdict. It was only as I was getting into bed last night that the truth flashed upon me. The gas was turned off by a murderer deliberately, *in order to show that the murder was not suicide.* It was a deliberate protest, an advertisement. Make what you like of this case (it seemed to say); but do not call it suicide; that at least is outside the scheme of possibilities.'

'Well, my solution was rather by way of allowing for that.'

'To be sure. But, you see, you involve yourself in a hopeless psychological improbability. You make a man commit suicide, leaving behind him an accomplice who will turn off the gas. Now, it's an extraordinary thing, our human love of interference, but I don't believe it's possible to have an accomplice in suicide. Except, of course, for those "death pacts" which we are all familiar with. Tell anyone that you mean to commit suicide, and that person will not only try to dissuade you, but will scheme to prevent your bringing the thing off. Suicide here would involve an accomplice; therefore it was not suicide. It was murder; and yet the murderer, so far from wanting to make it appear suicide, was particularly anxious to make it clear that it was *not* suicide. There is a strange situation for you.

'The strange situations, the mysterious situations, are not those which are most difficult to unravel. You can proceed in this case to look for the murderer in the certainty that he is someone who would stand to lose if a verdict of suicide were brought in. Puzzling it over last night, I was unable to conceive such a person. Between you and me, I had been inclined to suspect Brinkman; but there did not seem to be any possible reason why he should want to murder Mottram; and, if he did, there was no conceivable reason why he should want to make it appear that Mottram did not commit suicide. Brinkman was not the heir; the Euthanasia policy did not affect him.

'My discoveries of this morning put me on an entirely different track. There was one man in the world, and only one, whose interest bade him murder Mottram, and murder him in such a way that no suspicion of suicide could rest over the event. I mean, of course, young Simmonds. It was in his interest, as he must have thought, to murder Mottram, because if Mottram lived to be sixty-five the Euthanasia policy would run out. This was Simmonds' last chance but one, assuming that Mottram's yearly visits to Chilthorpe were the best chance of doing away with him. In two years from now, Mottram would have turned sixty-five, and the half-million would have vanished into the air. Moreover, there was much to be said for haste; who could tell when Mottram might not take it into his head to draw up a new will? As it seemed to Simmonds, he had only to get rid of this lonely, crusty old bachelor by a painless death, and he, as the next of kin, would walk straight into five hundred thousand. Meanwhile, there must be no suspicion of suicide; for any such suspicion might mean that your company would refuse to pay up, and the half-million would have disappeared once more.

'To young Simmonds, as he let himself in by the ground-floor casement into the "Load of Mischief", only one fear presented itself – the fear of a false verdict. He was of the type that cannot commit cold-blooded murder. The more civilization advances, the more ingenious does crime become; meanwhile, it becomes more and more difficult for one man to kill another with his hands. Simmonds might have been a poisoner; as it was, he had discovered a safer way; he would be a gasser. But there was this defect about the weapon he was using – it might create a false impression on the jury. Imperative, then, not merely to kill his man, but to prove that he had killed him. That is why, after turning on the gas in the sleeping man's room, he waited for two hours or so outside; then came back, flung open the window to get air, and turned the gas off again, only pausing to make sure that his victim was dead.

'How he worked the door trick I don't know. We shall find out later. Meanwhile, let me tell you that one of the friends I made last night in the bar-parlour told me he had seen Simmonds hanging round the hotel just after closing time, although (for the fellow is a teetotaller) he had not been drinking there. This was on the very night of the murder. That was a point in which I was in a position to score off you. There was another point, over which you had the same opportunities of information, but neglected them. You remember the letter which Mottram left lying about in his bedroom? It was in answer to a correspondent who signed himself "Brutus". I took the trouble to get, from the offices of the *Pullford Examiner*, a copy of the issue in which that letter appeared. It is a threatening letter, warning Mottram that retribution would come upon him for the bloodsucking methods by which his money had been made. And it was signed "Brutus" ... You've had a classical education; you ought to have spotted the point; personally I looked it up in an encyclopedia. Brutus wasn't merely a demagogue; he led the revolt in Rome which resulted in the expulsion of his own maternal uncle, King Tarquin. The same relation, you see, that there was between Simmonds and Mottram.

'Well, I've applied for a warrant. I'm in no hurry to use it; for, as long as Simmonds is off his guard, he's all the more likely to give himself away. Meanwhile, I'm having him watched. If you go and talk to him, just to form your own impressions, I know you'll be careful not to say anything which would give away my suspicions. And I can wait for that twenty pounds, too.'

Bredon sat spell-bound. He could see the whole thing happening; he could trace every calculation in the mind of the criminal. And yet he was not convinced. He was just about to explain this, when a fresh thought struck him and interfered with their session. 'Leyland,' he said, in a very quiet voice, 'you aren't smoking, and I've had my pipe out these last ten minutes. Can you tell me why there should be a smell of cigarette smoke?'

Leyland looked round, suddenly on the alert. It was only as he looked round that he noticed how insecure was their privacy. The rain had stopped some time since, and there was no reason why an interloper should not be standing outside, listening through one of the numerous chinks in the wall behind them. Gripping Bredon's arm, he darted out suddenly, and rounded the corner of the building. There was nobody there. But close to the wall lay a cigarette end, flattened and soiled as if it had been trodden out by a human foot. And as Leyland picked it up a faint spark and a thin stream of smoke showed that it had been trodden out only a moment before, not quite successfully. 'Callipoli,' he read, examining the stump. 'Not the sort of cigarette one buys in the village. It looks to me, Bredon, as if we were on the track of something fresh here. We'll leave that cigarette-stump exactly where we found it.'

CHAPTER II

The Generalship of Angela

'ANGELA,' said Bredon when he found her, 'I've got a job of work for you.'

'Such as?'

'All you've got to do is to make Brinkman and Pulteney open their cigarette-cases for inspection without knowing that they're doing it.'

'Miles, it won't do. You know I can't work in blinkers. There's nothing I dislike so much as a want of complete confidence between husband and wife. Sit down and tell me all about it. You'd better make sure of the door first.' And she turned down the little shutter which protected their keyhole on the inside.

'Oh, all right,' said Bredon, and told the story of their recent alarms. 'It almost must be somebody in the house. Brinkman and Pulteney are both cigarette-smokers, and of course it would be easy for me to cadge a cigarette by saying I'd run short. But that just might put the mysterious gentleman on his guard. And I don't want to hang about picking up fags. So what you've got to do is to lead round the conversation in such a way that we can have an opportunity of finding out what cigarettes each of them smokes, without his suspecting anything.'

'Why not pinch some from their rooms?'

'It might work. But since people took to smoking all kinds of vile cigarettes at the end of the war, one doesn't trouble to carry one's own brand about. One buys them at the local shop. These Callipolis are an oddity, but there probably aren't many more where they came from, and the safest place to look for them is inside somebody's breast-pocket. Anyhow, you might try.'

'Sort of salted almonds game?' said Angela reflectively. 'All right, I will. Don't you try your hand at it; sit there and back me up. Meanwhile you'd better go down and , have a pick-me-up at the bar, because I'm going to dress for dinner.'

'Dress for dinner, in a hole like this? Whatever for?'

'You don't understand the technique of the thing. If I'm to have complete control of the conversation, I must be looking my best. It makes all the difference with a susceptible old dear like Edward.'

She certainly had made herself look attractive, if a trifle exotic, by the time she came downstairs. The maid all but broke the soup-plates at the sight of her.

'Did you see much of Pullford, Mrs Bredon?' asked Brinkman, on hearing of their day's expedition.

'Much of it? Why, I'm practically a native of the place by now. I shall never see a perambulator again, I mean a drain-pipe, without a sort of homely feeling. My husband left me alone for three solid hours while he went and caroused with the hierarchy.'

'A very genial man, isn't he, the Bishop,' said Brinkman, appealing to her husband.

'What a poor compliment that word *genial* is,' put in the old gentleman. 'I would sooner be called well-meaning, myself. You have no grounds for saying that a man is really kind or charitable; you have not personally found him attractive; and yet he has a sort of good-natured way with him which demands some tribute. So you say he is genial.'

'Like a Dickens character?' suggested Brinkman.

'No, they are too human to be called merely genial. Mr Pickwick genial! It is like calling the Day of Judgement a fine sight. How did Pusey, by the way, ever have the wit to light upon such a comparison?'

'I think *witty* is rather a dreadful thing to be called,' said Angela. 'I always think of witty people as people who dominate the conversation with long anecdotes. How glad I am to have been born into a world in which the anecdote has gone out of fashion!'

'A hemisphere, Mrs Bredon,' said Brinkman in correction. 'You have not been to America? The anecdote there is in its first youth; the anecdotes mostly in their extreme old age.'

'There is a pleasant dryness about American humour,' objected Pulteney. 'But I confess that I miss piquancy in it.'

'Like Virginian tobacco?' suggested **Bredon**, and was rewarded by a savage kick from Angela under the table.

'The anecdote, however,' pursued Mr Pulteney, 'is the enemy of conversation. With its appearance, the shadow of egotism falls over our conviviality. The man who hoards up anecdotes, and lets them loose at intervals, is a social indecency; he might as well strip and parade some kind of acrobatic feat. See how your anecdotist lies in wait for his opportunity, prays for the moment that will lend excuse to his "That reminds me". There is a further pitch of shamelessness, at which such a man will assault you openly with: "Have you heard this one?" But, as long as men have some rags of behaviour left to them, your sex, Mrs Bredon, saves us from this conversational horror. When the ladies leave us, anecdotes flow out as from a burst dam.'

'That's because we don't know how to tell stories; we don't drag them out enough. When I try to tell a story, I always find I have got to the point when I've only just started.'

'You are too modest, Mrs Bredon. It is your essential altruism which preserves you. You women are always for helping out the conversation, not strangling it at birth. You humour us men, fool us to the top of our bent, yet you always restrain conversation from its worst extravagances – like a low organ accompaniment, you unobtrusively give us the note. All praise to your unselfishness.'

'I expect we are trained that way, or have trained ourselves that way. Civilization has taught us, perhaps, to play up to the men.'

'Indeed, no,' chirped Mr Pulteney, now thoroughly enjoying himself. 'Conversational receptivity is a natural glory of your sex. Nature itself, who bids the peacock strut to the admiration of the hen, bids you evoke the intellectual powers of the male. You flatter him by your attention, and he basks unconsciously in your approval. How much more knowledge of human nature had Virgil than Homer! Alcinous would never have got all that long story out of Ulysses; challenged by a direct question, the hero would probably have admitted, in a gruff voice, that he had been fooling around somewhere. It was a Dido that was needed to justify the hysteron proteron – *'multa super Priamo rogitans, super Hectore multa'*; she knew how to do it! But I become lyrical.'

'Do, please, be lyrical, Mr Pulteney. It's so good for Miles; he thinks he's a strong, silent man, and there's nothing more odious. The trouble is, of course, he thinks he's a kind of detective, and he has to play up to the part. Look at you, Mr Leyland, you've hardly uttered.'

'Is this helping us out in conversation, Mrs Bredon? You seem to be flogging us into it.'

'The strong silence of the detective,' explained the old gentleman, 'is a novelist's fiction. The novelist must gag his detective, or how is he to preserve his secret till the last chapter? No, it is Mr Brinkman who should be professionally silent; for what is a secretary if he does not keep secrets?'

'I am not silent, I am silenced,' said Brinkman. 'The second best peacock dare not strut, for fear of an encounter.'

'I find in silence,' said Bredon, 'a mere relief from the burden of conversation. I am grateful to the man who talks, as I should be grateful to the man who jumped in before me to rescue a drowning baby. He obviates the necessity for effort on my part. I sometimes think that is why I married.'

'Miles,' said Angela, 'if you are going to be odious, you will have to leave the room. I suppose you think you can be rude because the detectives in fiction are rude? Mr Leyland may be silent, but at least he's polite.'

'Mr Bredon is married,' suggested Pulteney. 'The caged bird does not strut. His are golden chains, I hasten to add, but they take the spring out of him none the less. For all that, I have some contempt for the man who does not take his share in shouldering the burden of conversation. He puts nothing into the common pot. Mr Brinkman, I resign the strutting-ground. Tell us whether you think detectives should be strong, silent men, or not.'

'I'm afraid I haven't read much in that direction, Mr Pulteney. I should imagine it was an advantage to the detective to be silent, so that he can be in a good position to say, "I told you so," when the truth comes out.'

'Oh, but a detective ought to be talking all the time,' protested Angela. 'The ones in the books always are. Only what they say is always entirely incomprehensible, both to the other people in the book and to the reader. "Let me call your attention once more," they say, "to the sinister significance of the bend in the toast-rack," and there you are, none the wiser. Wouldn't you like to be a detective, Mr Pulteney?'

'Why, in a sense I am.' There was a slight pause, with several mental gasps in it, till the old gentleman continued: 'That is to say, I am a schoolmaster; and the two functions are nearly akin. Who threw the butter at the ceiling, which boy cribbed from which, where the missing postage-stamp has got to –, these are the problems which agitate my inglorious old age. I do not know why headmasters allow boys to collect postage-stamps; they are invariably stolen.'

'Or why anybody wants to collect them?' suggested Angela. 'Some of them are quite pretty, of course. But I've no patience with all this pedantry about the exact date of issue, and the exact shape of the water-mark. But I suppose the water-mark helps you in your investigations, Mr Pulteney?'

'I am hardly professional enough for that. I leave that to the philatelist. A philatelist, by the way, means one who loves the absence of taxes. It hardly seems to mark out the stamp-lover from his fellows.'

'The detectives of fiction,' put in Leyland, 'are always getting important clues from the water-mark of the paper on which some cryptic document is written. That is where they have the luck. If you pick up the next four pieces of paper you see, and hold them up to the light, you will probably find that three of them have no water-mark at all.'

'I know,' said Angela. 'And I used to be told, when I was small, that every genuine piece of silver had a lion stamped on it. But of course they haven't really. I should think it's quite likely the wristwatch you gave me, Miles dear, has no lion on it.' She took it off as she spoke. 'Or it must be a teeny-weeny one if there is.'

'I think you're wrong there, Mrs Bredon.' It was

Brinkman who offered the correction. 'If you'll allow me to have a look at it... There, up there; it's a little rubbed away, but it's a lion all right.'

'I thought there always was a lion,' said Bredon, taking out a silver pencil-case with some presence of mind. 'Yes, this has got two, one passant and one cabinet size.'

'Let's see your watch, Mr Leyland,' suggested Angela, 'or is it electro?'

'It should be silver; yes, there's the little chap.' Immediately afterwards, Angela was rewarded by seeing Pulteney take a silver cigarette-case out of his pocket, and handing it over to her. 'It'll be on the inside of this, I suppose? Oh, no, it's all gilt stuff; yes, I see, here it is on the outside.' It is to be feared that she added 'Damn!' under her breath; the cigarette-case had been empty.

'I seem to be the only poor man present,' said Brinkman; 'I am all gun-metal.'

Angela did not trouble to influence the conversation further until the shape course was finished. Then, rather desperately, she said, 'Do smoke, Mr Leyland, I know you're dying to. What is a detective without his shag?' and was rewarded by seeing Brinkman take out the gun-metal case and light up. Mr Pulteney, after verifying his own cigarettelessness, began slowly to fill a briar.

Brinkman's cigarette, she had seen, was the last in the case; what if it should be the last of its box or of its packet? 'I wish I smoked,' she said. 'But if I did I would smoke a pipe; it always looks so comfortable. Besides, you can shut your eyes and go to sleep with a pipe, which must be rather dangerous with a cigarette.'

'You'd lose the taste of the pipe if you did,' objected Brinkman. 'It's an extraordinary thing, how little satisfaction you can get out of smoking in the dark.'

'Is that really true? I've always heard that about taste depending on sight, and not being able to distinguish one wine from another with one's eyes shut. Miles, if I put a handkerchief over your eyes, could you tell your beer from Mr Brinkman's cider? Oo, I say, let's try! I'll give them you in spoonfuls.'

'I'll shut my eyes and play fair,' suggested Bredon. The idiocy of men!

'No, you won't, you'll do what you're told. Anybody got a clean hanky? Thank you so much, Mr Leyland. ... There's that's right. Now, open your mouth, but not too wide, or you'll choke. ... Which was that?'

'Cider, I thought.'

'It was vinegar, really, with a little water in it.'

'Oh, shut up, that's not fair.' Miles tore away the handkerchief from his eyes. 'Hang it all, I won't strut; I'm a married man!'

'Then Mr Brinkman shall try instead; you will, won't you, Mr Brinkman?' It is to be feared that Angela favoured him with an appealing look; at any rate, he succumbed. With the instinct of the blindfolded man, he put his cigarette down on the edge of his plate. It was easy work for Angela to drop the spoon, and set Mr Pulteney grovelling for it. Meanwhile, she hastily picked up Brinkman's cigarette, and read the word 'Callipoli'.

CHAPTER 12

The Makings of a Trap

IT was Bredon and Leyland, this time, who took their evening walk together. To Bredon, events seemed to be closing in like a nightmare. Here was he pledged to uphold the theory of suicide; and he had depended largely for his success on Leyland's inability to produce a suitable candidate for the position of murderer. But now there seemed to be a perfect *embarras* of murderers. Macbeth wasn't in it.

'Well,' he said, 'at least we have something positive to go upon now. Brinkman's part in this business may be what you will, but he certainly takes an unhealthy interest in it, to the extent of hanging about round corners where he's no business to be. At least we can confront him with his behaviour, and encourage him to make a clean breast of the whole thing. I imagine you will have no objection to that, since it's not Brinkman you suspect of the murder?'

'I'm afraid,' said Leyland, 'that's not the way we go to work. The Force, I mean. It's quite true Brinkman is not the man I have under suspicion at the moment, but I'm only working on a theory, and that theory may prove to be a false one. I'm not certain of it yet, and I should have to be certain of it before I acquitted Brinkman.'

'But, hang it all, look at the question of motive. Simmonds, I grant you, had a reasonable motive for wanting to make away with his uncle. He had grounds for thinking that his uncle's death would mean a clear half-million to him. He had quarrelled with his uncle, and thought he had been treated badly. He disapproved of his uncle, and regarded him as a bloodsucker. The fact that Mottram was down at Chilthorpe was an excellent opportunity, and a rare opportunity, for young Simmonds to get at him. Seldom the time and the place and the hated one all together. But your Brinkman, as far as we can see, was only affected by the death in the sense that he has lost a good job and has now to look out for another one, with no late employer to supply him with testimonials. Personally, I believe Brinkman did know about the alteration in the will; at least he knew about the uncertainty of Mottram's health. Can you suppose that, even if Simmonds offered to go halves with him, he would consent to be an accomplice in what might prove a wholly unnecessary crime?'

'You're assuming too much. We don't know yet that Brinkman has no financial interest in the affair. Look here – this is far-fetched, I grant you, but it's not impossible. Everybody says Mottram had no family; whose word have they for that except his own? Where did he pick up Brinkman? No one knows. Why did he want a secretary? There was some talk of writing a history of Pullford, but nothing ever came of it. Why, then, this curious interest which Mottram takes in Brinkman? I don't say it's likely, but I say it's possible that Brinkman is Mottram's son by a clandestine marriage. If that's so, and if Brinkman didn't know about the codicil, he may himself be the next of kin who is preparing to step into the half-million. And a clever man – Brinkman is a clever man – might find it convenient to get Mottram out of the way, and get someone else to do it for him. He is afraid that Mottram will live to be sixty-five, and the policy will leave no benefits behind it. Or he is afraid that Mottram is going to make a new will. What does he do? Why, he goes to Simmonds, and points out to him that as the next of kin he would score by putting Mottram through it. Simmonds does so, all unsuspecting; and here's Brinkman, only waiting to step in and claim the half-million on the strength of his mother's marriage-lines!'

'You're too confoundedly ingenious. Things don't happen like that.'

'Things have happened like that before now, and with less than half a million to give grounds for them. No, I'm not going to leave Brinkman out of my calculations, and therefore I'm not going to take him into my confidence. But this eavesdropping of his does give us a very important chance, and we're going to use it.'

'I don't quite see how.'

'That's because you're not a professional, and you don't

know the way things are done in the Force. The outside
public doesn't, and we don't mean it to. We don't show
our workings. But half, or say a third at least, of the big
businesses we clear up are cleared up by bluff, by leading
the suspected man on and encouraging him to give himself away. Sometimes it isn't a very pretty business, of
course; we have to use agents who are none too scrupulous.
But here we've got a ready-made chance of bluffing our
man, and bluffing him into betraying himself.'

'How, exactly?'

'You and I are going to meet again in that mill-house.
And we are going to talk about it openly beforehand, so
that we can be jolly sure Brinkman will creep up behind
and listen to us. And when we've got him comfortably
fixed there listening to us, you and I are going to lead him
up the garden. We are going to make him overhear
something which is really meant for his ears, though he
thinks it's meant for anybody's ears rather than his own.'

'Oh, I see ... a fake conversation. I say, I'm not much
of an actor. Angela would do it far better than I should.'

'There's no acting wanted. All you've got to do is to sit
there and argue pig-headedly about its being suicide, the
same as you always do. Meanwhile, I'll do the fake part –
or rather, it won't be much of a fake, either. I shall repeat
what I told you yesterday, about suspecting Simmonds.
That's all true enough; I do suspect the man; though I
wish he wasn't so confoundedly innocent and self-possessed
under examination. Then I shall say that I also suspect
Brinkman – not letting on, of course, about the cigarette
and all that, but putting up some ground or other for
suspicion. Simmonds, I shall say, is clearly the murderer,
but I've reason to think Brinkman knows more about it
than he ought to do. I shall say that I'm going to have
Brinkman shadowed, and that I'm going to get a warrant
for his arrest. At the same time, I shall say I think he's a
fool not to own up, if his share in the business is not a
guilty one. And so on. Then we just wait and see how
Brinkman reacts.'

'I should think he'd skip.'

'That's what I want him to do. Of course, I've got him
shadowed already. If he makes a determined bolt for it,

that gives me reasonable ground for putting him under arrest.'

'What else can he do?'

'Well, if he's relatively innocent, he might confide in you about it.'

'Oh, I see, that's the game. Damn it, why did I ever consent to become a spy? Leyland, I don't like this job. It's too – too underhand.'

'Well, you were an intelligence officer, weren't you? There was no trick you wouldn't play, while the war was on, to beat the Germans. Why should you be more squeamish about it when you've the well-being of Society to consider? Your job is to protect the interests of all the honest men who've insured with your Company. My business is to see that harmless people don't get gassed in their sleep. In any case, we've got to get at the truth. I might even point out that we've got a bet on it.'

'But look here, if Brinkman confides in me, am I to betray his confidence? That hardly seems cricket.'

'Well, if you're not a fool, you'd better avoid making any promise of secrecy. You must act up to your own confounded conscience, I suppose. But remember, Brinkman can't get away; I've got him watched all right. If his part in the show is quite an innocent one, you'd better point out to him that his best plan is to make a clean breast of it.'

'Well, I'll help you bait the trap. If Brinkman comes to me about it, I can't answer for what I'll do – unless you subpoena me, of course. By the way, what happens if Brinkman doesn't react at all? If he simply does nothing about it?'

'We shall be just where we were before. But I think if we give him a lead he's almost certain to take it. After all, there's no reason why he should stay on here, but he hasn't shown any signs of moving yet. Once the funeral's over, he'll be anxious to put things straight, if only to get a fresh job.'

By now they were on their return journey, on the road leading down the valley; the twilight was gathering, and the few street-lamps which Chilthorpe afforded had not yet been lit. It was but natural that on a summer evening such a road as this should be a trysting-place of lovers.

There is a sentimental streak in all our natures which warns us that a young man and a young woman sharing a railway carriage must be left to share it; and equally that a pair of lovers in a lane must be passed by as hastily as possible, with no inquisitive looks thrown in their direction. It is our instinct thus to propitiate the Paphian Queen. It was characteristic of Bredon that, as he passed one of these couples from behind, seeing their heads close together in earnest colloquy, he quickened his pace and never looked backwards. It was equally characteristic of Leyland that although he, too, quickened his pace, he did let his eye rest on the pair for a moment – lightly, it seemed, and uncomprehendingly. But when they were out of earshot he showed that his had been no casual glance.

'You saw them, Bredon, eh? You saw them?'

'I saw there were some people there. I didn't–'

'You wouldn't. But it doesn't do to miss these things. The young lady is the barmaid at our hotel, the lady who always says "Raight-ho!" when you ask for anything. And the young man is our friend Mr Simmonds. It looks as if a *mésalliance* were in contemplation, from the Simmonds point of view. And it means – well, it may mean almost anything.'

'Or almost nothing.'

'Well, if you ask me, it seems to be a matter of some importance to know that Simmonds has got his foot inside the door, so to speak, at the "Load of Mischief". He had somebody there to let him in and let him out late at night. He had somebody to cover his traces, if necessary, when the crime was over. I think our nets are beginning to close at last.'

'Like to hide behind the hedge and listen to what they're saying?'

'Why, it might be done. But it seemed to me they had their voices lowered all the time, not merely while we were passing. No, I think it's the bar parlour for me.'

Angela was far more enthusiastic than her husband over the proposed ambush. 'You see, Brinky can't really be a very nice man, or he wouldn't have been listening at our keyhole. Just think, I might have been ticking you off about your table-manners or something. No, if he will go and hide in the arras he must take what he gets, like Polonius. And after all, if he does come to you afterwards and wants to sob on your bosom, you can always refuse to promise secrecy. The world would be such a much happier place if people wouldn't make promises.'

'None at all?'

'Don't be soppy. You aren't in the Lovers' Lane now. Meanwhile, I think it would be a good thing if you overcame your natural *bonhomie*, and had a talk with Mr Simmonds tomorrow. The more necessary, since you only seem to have brought three hankies here, and it's you for the haberdasher's in any case.'

'All right; but you mustn't come. You cramp my style in shops. Too much of the I-want-a-handkerchief-for-this-young-gentleman business about you.'

'Then I shall console myself by talking to the barmaid, and finding out if she's capable of saying anything except "Raight-ho". Of course, I knew she had a young man all the time.'

'Rot! How could you tell?'

'My dear Miles, no girl ever waits so badly as that, or tosses her head like that, unless she's meaning to chuck up her job almost immediately. I deduced a young man.'

'I wonder you haven't wormed yourself into her confidence already.'

'Wasn't interested in her. But tonight, at supper, she was jumpy – even you must have noticed it. She almost dropped the soup-plates, and the shape was quivering like a guilty thing surprised.'

'That was your dressing for dinner.'

'Bunkum. You must have seen that she was all on edge. Anyhow, we're going to have a heart-to-heart talk.'

'All right. Don't bully the wretched girl, though.'

'Miles! You really mustn't go running after every woman you meet like this. I shall deal with her with all my well-known delicacy and tact. Look how I managed them at supper! I should have cried, I think, if I'd found it was Edward who smoked the "Callipoli". Do you think Leyland has still got his knife into Simmonds? Or do you think he wants to arrest Brinky, and is only using Simmonds as a blind?'

'He was excited enough when we met Simmonds in the lane. No, I think he's out to arrest everybody at the moment; Simmonds for doing the murder, and Brinkman for persuading him or helping him to do it. He's got 'em both shadowed, anyhow, he says – I hope not by the Chilthorpe police, who look to me too substantial to be mistaken for shadows. But I'm sure I'm right, I'm sure I'm right.'

'Of course you are. Though, mind you, it looks to me as if Mottram had only just managed to commit suicide in time to avoid being murdered. The trouble about Leyland's Simmonds theory is that it makes the little man too clever. I don't believe Leyland could ever catch a criminal unless he were a superhumanly clever criminal; and of course, so few of them are. They go and make one rotten little mistake, and so get caught out.'

'You're getting too clever. It's quite time you went to bed.'

'Raight-ho, as your friend the barmaid says. No, don't stamp about and pretend to be a cave-man. Go downstairs like a good boy, and help Leyland incriminate the Oldest Inhabitant. He'll be getting to that soon.'

CHAPTER 13

A Morning with the Haberdasher

THE sun rose bright the next morning, as if it had heard there was a funeral in contemplation, and was determined to be there. The party at the 'Load of Mischief' rose considerably later, and more or less coincided at the break-fast-table. 'I am afraid we shall be losing you?' said Mr Pulteney to Angela. 'A fortunate crime privileged us with your presence; when the mortal remains of it have been put away, I suppose that your husband's work here is done? Unless, of course, Mrs Davis's eggs and bacon have determined you to stay on here as a holiday.'

'I really don't know what we are doing, Mr Pulteney. My husband, of course, will have to write a report for those tiresome people at the office, and that will take a little time. Why do men always take a whole day to write a report? I don't suppose we shall be leaving till to-morrow in any case. Perhaps you will have caught a fish by then.'

'If you would only consent to stay till that happens, we should all congratulate ourselves. But, seriously, it will be a deprivation. I came to this hotel feeling that I was fore-doomed to solitude, or the company, now and again, of a stray bagman. Instead, I have found the place a feast of reason; and I shall regret the change.'

'You'll still have Mr Brinkman.'

'What is Brinkman? A man who cannot tell beer from cider with his eyes shut. ... Ah, here he is. I have been lamenting the loss Mr and Mrs Bredon will be to our desert island. But you, too, I suppose, will be for Pullford again before the funeral bakemeats are cold?'

'Me? Oh, I don't know. ... My plans are rather vague. The house at Pullford is almost shut up; everybody except the housekeeper away. I daresay I shall stay on a bit, and then, I suppose, go to London to look for another job.'

'With better auspices, I hope. Well, you deserve a rest before you settle down to the collar again. Talking of collars' (he addressed himself to the barmaid, who had just come in with more eggs and bacon), 'I wonder if you could represent to Mrs Davis the desirability of sending some of my clothes to the wash?'

'Raight-ho,' said the barmaid, unconcernedly.

'I thank you; you gratify my least whim. Ah, here is Mr Leyland! I trust you have slept off the weariness induced by the coroner's allocution yesterday?'

'Quite, thanks,' said Leyland, grinning. 'Good morning, Mrs Bredon. Good-morning, Bredon; I wonder if you could give me ten minutes or a quarter of an hour after breakfast? ... No, no porridge, thanks; just eggs and bacon.'

'Yes, rather. We might stroll back to the mill-house, if you don't mind, for I rather think I dropped a packet of pipe-papers there. In fact, I think I'll go on there and wait for you. No hurry.'

It was some twenty minutes before Leyland turned up, and almost at the moment of his arrival both men heard a very faint click behind them, as if somebody on the further side of the wall, in walking gently, had dislodged a loose stone. They exchanged an instantaneous glance, then Leyland opened up the prearranged conversation. There was something curiously uncanny about this business of talking entirely for the benefit of a concealed audience, but they both carried off the situation creditably.

'Well,' began Bredon, 'you're still hunting for murderers?'

'For a murderer, to be accurate. It doesn't take two men to turn on a gas-jet. And when I say I'm hunting for him, I'm not exactly doing that; I'm hunting him. The motive's clear enough, and the method's clear enough, apart from details, but I want to make my case a little stronger before I take any action.'

'You've applied for a warrant, you say?'

'Against Simmonds, yes. At least, I wrote last night, though of course with the posts we have here it won't reach London till this evening, and probably late this evening. Meanwhile, I keep him under observation.'

'You're still sure he's your man?'

'I can hardly imagine a stronger case. There's the

motive present, and a good motive, too, half a million pounds. There's the disposition, a natural resentment against his uncle for treating him hardly, added to a conscientious objection to his great wealth and the means by which he made it. There's the threat; that letter of "Brutus" will tell in a law-court, if I know anything of juries. There's the occasion, the fact of Mottram happening to be down at Chilthorpe. There's the facility – we know that he was hand-in-glove with the barmaid, who could let him in at any hour of the day or night, who could further his schemes, and cover his traces. Finally, there is the actual coincidence of his whereabouts; I can bring testimony to prove that he was hanging round the "Load of Mischief" at a time when all honest teetotallers ought to be in bed. There's only one thing more that I want, and only one thing on the other side that would make me hold my hand.'

'What's the one thing you want?'

'Definite evidence to connect him with the actual room in which Mottram was sleeping. If he'd dropped anything there, so much as a match-head; if he'd left even a finger-mark about anywhere, I'd have the noose round his neck. But if you haven't got just that last detail of evidence, juries are often slow to convict. I could tell you of murderers who are at large now simply because we couldn't actually connect them with the particular scene of the crime, or with the particular weapon the crime was committed with.'

Bredon could not help admiring the man. It was obvious that he was still allowing for the possibility of Brinkman's guilt, and was accordingly advising Brinkman, whom he knew to be hidden round the corner, to manufacture some clue which would point to Simmonds, and thereby to give himself away. Bredon could not help wondering whether this was the real purpose of the colloquy, and whether he himself was not being kept in the dark. However, he had his sailing orders, and continued to play up to them.

'And the one thing which would make you hold your hand?'

'Why, if I could get satisfactory proof that Simmonds

knew of the existence of that codicil. You see, *we* know that
Simmonds did not stand to gain anything by murdering
his uncle, because, in fact, his uncle had signed away all
his expectations to the Bishop of Pullford. Now, if I could
feel certain that Simmonds knew where he stood; knew
that there was nothing coming to him as next of kin –
why, then the motive would be gone, and with the motive
my suspicions. The fact that he disliked his uncle, the fact
that he disapproved of his uncle, wouldn't make him
murder his uncle. It's a humiliating fact, but you don't
ever get a crime of this sort without some *quid pro quo* in
the form of hard cash. If I felt sure that Simmonds knew
he was cut out of the will altogether, then I'd acquit him,
or be prepared to acquit him. If, on the other hand, somebody could produce good reason for thinking that Simmonds was expecting to profit by his uncle's will, then my
case would be proportionately strengthened.'

Once more Bredon listened with admiration. The man
who was concealed behind the wall had been Mottram's
own secretary, more likely than any other man living to
know how the facts stood. And Leyland was appealing to
him, if he had any relevant knowledge about Simmonds'
expectations, to produce it; if he had none, to forge it, and
thereby give himself away. The game began to thrill him
in spite of himself.

'And, meanwhile, what of our other friend?'

'Brinkman? Well, as I told you, I don't suspect Brinkman directly. He had no motive for the crime, as far as we
can see. But he is not playing the game, and for the life
of me I can't think why. For instance, he has been ready
from the first to back up your idea of suicide. In fact, it
seems to have been he who first mentioned the word
suicide in connexion with this business. He told you, for
example, that he thought Dr Ferrers must have shut off
the main gas-jet by accident. He said, I think you told me,
that it was very loose. As a matter of fact, it was very stiff
at the time, and he must have known that it was stiff; for
it was he who borrowed a pair of pincers for me when I
wanted to loosen it. And there are some other bits of
evidence, which I'm afraid I'm not at liberty to mention
to you, which make me look askance at Brinkman's

behaviour. He's hiding something, but what?'

'I don't see what good he can be doing himself by holding back.'

'Precisely. I don't want to injure the fellow, but I must get at the truth. I'm writing tonight for a warrant; not because I think he's the guilty man, but because we must get his evidence somehow, and I think a taste of prison detention might make him speak out. But of course it's bad luck on the fellow, because a record like that, however much he is cleared, is bound to count against him when he looks out for a new job. It's possible that he's shielding Mottram's reputation, or it's possible that he's afraid of coming under suspicion himself, or it's possible that he's simply lost his head, and, having no one to consult, can't make up his mind what to do. But he's cutting his own throat; there's no doubt about that. I can't think he's really guilty, or why hasn't he skipped? For all we could do, he could be in Vienna in a couple of days, and we none the wiser. Yet he stays on, and stays on as if there was some end to be gained by it.'

.'But if he went off you could arrest him on suspicion, couldn't you?'

'Could I? Hardly, on what I know at present. I'm looking forward, you see, to Simmonds' evidence when he's arrested. I know that type, anaemic, nervous; once he's arrested, with any luck we can make him tell us the whole story: and then, if Brinkman really has been up to anything, it will be too late for him to get clear. But, as I say, I don't believe Brinkman is a wrong 'un. If only he'd have the sense to confide in me – or in you, if he's afraid of the police. ... Well, I wanted to tell you all this, so that you'll know where you are in dealing with Simmonds. Mrs Bredon told me you were hoping to get a look at him today.'

'That's the idea. To tell the truth, I think I'd better be starting now, because it's easier to have a private interview with him if I go into the shop before the rush hour begins. Not that the rush hour at Chilthorpe is likely to be very formidable, but I don't want to have our *tête-à-tête* interrupted by old ladies matching ribbons.'

Bredon strolled off. Leyland stayed where he was till he

guessed the coast would be clear, and then went cautiously round to the back of the building. He found what he had expected, and hoped for. The cigarette, which they had left the night before in the place where it lay, had by now been carefully removed.

When Bredon reached the shop, he found that Fortune was smiling on him. There seemed to be only one attendant about besides Simmonds himself, and this was a freckled, sandy-haired youth who was cleaning the front windows with every appearance of deliberation. Nor were there any rival shoppers so early on a Chilthorpe morning. Mr Simmonds approached the handkerchief question with the air of being just the right man to come to. Other things, you felt, were to be bought in this shop; teethers, for example, and walking-sticks, and liquorice, and so on. But when you came to *handkerchiefs*, there you had found a specialist, a man who had handled handkerchiefs these fifteen years past. Something stylish, perhaps, was required? This with a glance at the customer, as if to size him up and recognize the man of taste. 'The *plain* ones? Just plain white, you mean, Sir? Well, it's a curious thing, but I'm not certain I can lay my hand on one of them. You see, there's more demand for the coloured ones, a bit of edging, anyhow. And, you see, we haven't got in our new stock yet.' (They never have got in their new stock yet at Simmonds'.) 'Three weeks ago, I could have done you a very good line in the plain ones, but I'm rather afraid we're right out. I'll just see.'

This was followed by an avalanche of drawers, containing handkerchiefs of every conceivable variety that was not plain. A violent horse-shoe pattern, that ran through all the gamut of the colours; a kind of willow pattern; a humorous series featuring film stars; striped edges, spotted edges, check edges – but no plain. From time to time Mr Simmonds would draw attention to the merits of the exhibits, as if it were just his luck that his customer should be a man so unadventurous in taste. 'Now, that's a very good number; you couldn't get a better line than that, not if it was a coloured handkerchief you were wanting. ... No, no, Sir, no trouble at all; I daresay perhaps I may be able to lay my hand on the article you require. ... You

don't fancy those, now? Those come very cheap because
they're bankrupt stock. Just you feel that, Sir, and see
what a lot of wear there is in it. ... Yes, that's right,
they're a little on the gay side, Sir. But we don't get any
real demand, not for the plain ones; people don't seem to
fancy them nowadays. Mind you, if you'll be staying on
here for a day or two, I could get you some; we shall be
sending into Pullford the day after tomorrow. But at the
moment we seem to be right out of them. ... Oh, you'll
take the check ones ... half a dozen? Thank you, Sir;
you'll find they're a very good line; you could go a long
way and not find another handkerchief just like that one.
It's a handkerchief we've stocked many years now, and
never had any difficulty in getting rid of it. And the next
article, please?'

But Bredon did not meditate any more purchases. He
had begun to realize that in Chilthorpe you bought, not
the thing you wanted, but the thing Mr Simmonds had in
stock. As the parcel was being wrapped up, he sat down
on a high, uncomfortable chair close to the counter, and
opened conversation about the deceased. Simmonds
might have quarrelled with his uncle, but surely he would
take the gloomy pride of the uneducated in his near
relationship to a corpse.

'I'm afraid you've had a sad loss, Mr Simmonds.'

Now, why did the man suddenly turn a white, haggard
face towards his visitor, starting as if the remark had been
something out of the way? There was no secret about the
relationship; it had been mentioned publicly at the inquest. Leyland had insisted that in all his interviews with
Simmonds he had failed to observe any sign of discom-
posure. Yet this morning a mere allusion to Mottram
seemed to throw his nephew all out of gear! The cant
phrases of his craft had flowed from him mechanically
enough, but once his customer began to talk the gossip of
the village, all the self-possession fell from him like a mask,
and he stood pale and quivering.

'As you say, Sir. Very melancholy event. My uncle, Sir,
he was. Oh, yes, Sir. We didn't see him much down here –
we hadn't anything to do with him, Sir. We didn't get on
very well – what I mean is, he didn't think much of me.

No, Sir. But he was my uncle, Sir. Over in Pullford he lived; hasn't lived here for many years now, though it was his own place.'

'Still, blood's thicker than water, isn't it?'

'What's that, Sir? Oh, I see what you mean, yes, Sir. I'm seeing to the funeral and all that. Excuse me one moment, Sir. Sam! Just take a pair of steps and put them boxes back, there's a good lad. And there's nothing else today, Sir?'

There was nothing else. Bredon had meant to say a good deal, but he had reckoned on dealing with a smug, self-possessed tradesman, who might unsuspectingly drop a few hints that were worth knowing. Instead, he found a man who started at shadows, who was plainly alive with panic. He went back to his hotel full of disquiet; there went his twenty pounds, and the Company's half-million. And yet, what did it all mean? Why did Simmonds tremble in the presence of Bredon, when he had shown no trace of embarrassment in talking to Leyland, who was an official of the police? The whole tangle of events seemed to become more complicated with every effort that was made to unravel it.

CHAPTER 14

Bredon is Taken for a Walk

IN front of the 'Load of Mischief' stands an alehouse
bench – that is the description which leaps to the mind.
Ideally, it should be occupied by an old gaffer in a white
smock, drinking cider and smoking a churchwarden pipe.
A really progressive hotel would hire a gaffer by the day
to do it. A less appropriate advertisement, yet creditable
enough to the establishment in the bright air of the June
morning, Angela was occupying this seat as her husband
came back from his shopping; she was knitting in a nice,
old-fashioned way, but spoilt the effect of it rather by
whistling as she did so.

'Well, did you get a bargain?' she asked.

'So I am assured. I have got a very good line; I could
go a long way and not find another handkerchief just like
this one. Or indeed six other handkerchiefs just like these
six. They are distinctive, that is the great point. Even you,
Angela, will have difficulty in getting them lost at the
wash.'

'And how was Mr Simmonds?' asked Angela, dropping her voice.

Bredon looked round cautiously. But Angela had chosen
her place well; she knew that publicity is the surest safe-
guard of privacy. In the open square in front of the inn,
nobody would suppose that you were exchanging anything but trivialities. Bredon communicated his mystifi-
cation and his alarm, depicting the strange behaviour of
the haberdasher in terms that left no room for doubt.

'Yes,' said Angela when he had finished, 'you were
quite right not to press him with any more questions. It
would only have put the wind up him. You do seem to be
rather heavy-handed, somehow, over these personal jobs.
Now, I've been having it out with Raight-ho since breakfast, and I got quite a lot out of her. Miles, that girl's a
jewel. If she wasn't going to be married, I'd get her to
come to Burrington, in spite of your well-known suscep-

98

tibility. But it's no use; the poor girl is determined to sign
away her liberty!'

'To Mr Simmonds?'

'So I gather, from what Mr Leyland told me last night.
But, of course, I was far too discreet to ask for any names.'

'How did you manage to worm yourself into her confidence? I'd as soon tackle a stone wall.'

'One must unbend. It's easier for us women. By a
sudden inspiration, I reflected that it must be an awful
nuisance washing up all those plates after breakfast,
especially in a pub where they seldom have more than
two guests at a time. So I offered to help. That was just
about the time you went out shopping. I'm quite good at
washing up plates, you know, thanks to having married
beneath me. She said, "Raight-ho", and we adjourned
to the scullery, where I did wonders. In the scullery I saw
a copy of *Home Hints*, which was very important.'

'I don't quite see why.'

'Don't you remember that cantankerous old bachelor
friend of yours who came to us once in London, Soames, I
think his name was, who told us that he wrote the column
headed Cupid's Labyrinth? The column that gives advice
to correspondents, you know, about affairs of the heart.
It's the greatest mistake in the world to suppose that the
modern pillion-girl is any less soppy about her amours
than the young misses of last century. I knew instinctively
that Raight-ho – her name, by the way, is Emmeline, poor
thing – was an avid reader of Cupid's Labyrinth. And
I'm afraid I rather prevaricated.'

'Angela, you surprise me. What particular form of lie
did you blacken your soul with this time?'

'Oh, I didn't exactly *say* anything. But I somehow
allowed her to get the impression that it was I who did the
column. After all, Mr Soames is a friend of yours, so it
wasn't so very far from the truth. Miles, she rose to the
bait like anything.'

'Heaven forgive you! Well, go on.'

'It was all to save you twenty quid, after all. Up till
then, she'd been saying all the ordinary things – she'd got
a sister in London, whom she goes and stays with; and she
finds Chilthorpe rather slow, hardly ever going to the

pictures, and that; and she'd like to get up to London herself – it's what they all say. But when I let on that I was Aunt Daphne of Cupid's Labyrinth, she spread herself. How would I advise a friend of hers to act, who found herself in a very delicate situation? So I told her to cough it up. The friend, it seemed, had been walking out with a young man who was quite decently off, that is, he had quite enough to marry on. But one day he explained to her that he had expectations of becoming really very rich, if only a relation of his would die; he would then come into a property far above his own station, let alone hers.'

'The situation sounds arresting, in more ways than one.'

'Don't interrupt. Well, the man suggested they should get engaged, and they did, only on the quiet. And then, a few weeks ago, or it might have been a fortnight ago, this man suddenly informed her friend that all his dreams of wealth had suddenly collapsed. The rich relation had made a new will, in which he made no provision for his family. And he, the young man, was very nice about it; and said of course he'd asked her to marry him at a time when he thought he could make her a rich woman; and now he couldn't. So if she wanted to back out of the engagement now, he would give her complete liberty.'

'Sportsman.'

'Her friend indignantly said No; she wouldn't dream of backing out. She wanted to marry him for himself, not for his money, and all that. So they are continuing to regard the engagement as a fixture. But her difficulty, I mean the friend's difficulty, is this – was it just a sort of melodramatic instinct which made her say that the money meant nothing to her? Was it just her pride which made her think she was still in love with the man, now that he was no longer an heir? Or was she really still in love with him? That was the problem, and I had to set to and answer it.'

'And what was your answer?'

'Oh, that's hardly important, is it? Of course, I put on my best Aunt Daphne manner, and tried to think of the sort of tripe Soames would have written. It wasn't difficult, really. I said that if the man was quite comfortably off as it was, it was probably far better for them both that they shouldn't become enormously rich; and I laid it on thick about the deceitfulness of riches, though I wish I'd more experience of it, don't you? And I said if they were already walking out before the man mentioned anything about the legacy, that proved that her friend was already in love with him, or half in love with him, before the question of money cropped up at all. And I told her I thought her friend would be very happy with the man, probably all the happier because he knew that she wasn't mercenary in her ambitions. And all that sort of thing – I felt rather a beast doing it. She was very grateful, and it didn't seem to occur to her for a moment that she was giving herself away, horse, foot, and guns. She can't have known, obviously, that you and Leyland were rubbering in the lane last night. And so there it is.'

'And confoundedly important at that. Angela, you are a trump! We've got Leyland down, both ears touching. He himself said that his theory about Simmonds would break down if it could be proved that Simmonds did know about the codicil, did know that he'd been cut out of the will. And it can be proved; we can prove it! It's too much of a coincidence, isn't it, that all this should have happened a fortnight ago or thereabouts? Obviously it was hearing about the codicil which made Simmonds offer to free Raight-ho from her engagement, and jolly sporting of him, I consider.'

'Candour compels me to admit that I've been rather efficient. But, Miles dear, the thing doesn't make sense yet. We know now that Simmonds wasn't expecting anything from his uncle's will, and therefore had no motive for murdering him, unless it was mere spite. Then why has Simmonds got the wind up so badly? You aren't as frightening as all that.'

'Yes; it still looks as if Simmonds had got something on his mind. And we know Brinkman's got something on his mind. Perhaps Brinkman will react on this morning's conversation, and let us know a little more about it.'

Almost as he spoke, Brinkman came out from the door of the inn. He came straight up to Bredon as if he had been looking for him, and said: 'Oh, Mr Bredon, I was wondering if you would care to come for a bit of a walk. I shall get no exercise this afternoon, with the funeral to attend, and I thought perhaps you'd like a turn round the gorge. It's considered rather a local feature, and you oughtn't to leave without seeing it.'

It was clumsily done. He seemed to ignore Angela's presence, and pointedly excluded her, with his eyes, from the invitation. It seemed evident that the man was determined on a *tête-à-tête*. Angela's glance betrayed a surprise which she did not feel, and perhaps a pique which she did, but she rose to the occasion. 'Do take him out, Mr Brinkman. He's getting dreadfully fat down here. Instead of taking exercise, he comes out and chats to me in public, more like a friend than a husband – and he's making me drop my stitches.'

'Aren't *you* coming?' asked Bredon, with a wholly unnecessary wink.

'Not if I know it. I'm not dressed for gorge-inspecting. You may buy me a picture-postcard of it, if you like, on the way back.'

The two strolled off up the valley. Bredon's heart beat fast; it was evident that Brinkman was taking advantage of the overheard conversation, and was preparing to make some kind of disclosure. Was he at last on the track of the secret? Well, he must be careful not to betray himself by any leading questions. The pose of the amiable incompetent, which he had already sustained with Brinkman, would do well enough.

'It's a fine thing, the gorge,' said Brinkman. 'It lies just below the Long Pool; but fortunately Pulteney isn't fishing the Long Pool today, so we shan't be shouted at and told to keep away from the bank. I really think, apart from the fishing, Chilthorpe is worth seeing, just for the gorge. Do you know anything about geology and such things?'

'You can search me. Beats me how they do it.'

'It beats me how the stream does it. Here's a little trickle of water, that can't shift a pebble weighing half a pound. Give it a few thousand years, and it eats its way through the solid rock, and digs a course for itself a matter of fifteen or twenty feet deep. And all that process is a mere moment of time, compared with the millions of years that lie behind us. If you want to reckon the age of the earth's crust, they say, you must do it in thousands of millions of years. Queer, isn't it?'

'Damned rum.'

'You almost understate the position. Don't you feel, sometimes, as if the whole of human life on this planet were a mere episode, and all our boasted human achievement were a speck on the ocean of infinity?'

'Sometimes. But one can always take a pill, can't one?'

'Why, yes, if it comes to that. ... An amusing creature, Pulteney.'

'Bit high-brow, isn't he? He always makes me feel rather as if I were back at school again. My wife likes him, though.'

'He has the school-master's manner. It develops the conversational style, talking to a lot of people who have no chance of answering back. You get it with parsons, too, sometimes. I really believe it would be almost a disappointment to him if he caught a fish, so fond is he of satirizing his own performance. ... You haven't been in these parts before, have you?'

'Never. It's a pity, really, to make their acquaintance in such a tragic way. Gives you a kind of depressing feeling about a place, when your first introduction to it is over a death-bed.'

'I am sure it must. ... It's a pity the country out towards Pullford has been so much spoilt by factories. It used to be some of the finest country in England. And there's nothing like English country, is there? Have you travelled much, apart from the war, of course?'

'Now, what the devil does this man think he's doing?' Bredon asked himself. Could it be that Brinkman, after making up his mind to unbosom himself, was feeling embarrassed about making a start, was taking refuge in every other conceivable topic so as to put off the dreaded moment of confession? That seemed the only possible construction to put on his conversational vagaries. But how to give him a lead? 'Very little, as a matter of fact. I suppose you went about a good deal with Mottram? I should think a fellow as rich as he was gets a grand chance of seeing the world. Funny his wanting to spend his holiday in a poky little place like this.'

'Well, I suppose each of us has his favourite corner of earth. There, do you see how deep the river has cut its way into the rock?'

They had left the road by a foot-path, which led down steeply through a wood of fir-trees and waist-deep bracken to the river bank. They were now looking up a deep gully, it almost seemed a funnel, of rock; both sides falling sheer from the tumbled boulders and fern-tufts of the hillside. Before them, a narrow path had been worn or cut out of the rock face, some five or six feet above the brawling stream, just clear of the foam that sprang from its sudden waterfalls. There was no habitation of men in view; the roaring of the water drowned the voice unless you shouted; the sun, so nearly at its zenith, could not reach the foot of the rocks, and the gorge itself looked gloomy and a little eerie from the contrast. 'Let's go along the path a bit,' said Brinkman; 'one gets the effect of it better when one's right in the middle of it. The path,' he explained, 'goes all the way along, and it's the regular way by which people go up when they mean to fish the Long Pool. I'll go first, shall I?'

For a second Bredon hesitated. The man had so obviously been making conversation all the way, had so obviously been anxious to bring him to this particular spot, that he suddenly conceived the idea of hostile design. A slight push, disguised as an effort to steady you round a corner, might easily throw you off the path into the stream; they were alone, and neither rock nor stream, in such an event, would readily give up its secret. Then he felt the impossibility of manufacturing any excuse for refusing the invitation. Brinkman, too, was a good foot smaller than himself.

'All right,' he said, 'I'll follow on.' He added a mental determination to follow at a safe distance.

About twenty yards from the entrance, they stopped at a resting-place where the rock-path widened out till it was some five feet in breadth. Behind it was a smooth face of rock six or seven feet in height, a fresh narrow ledge separating it from the next step in that giant's stairway.

'Curious, ain't it,' said Brinkman, 'the way these rocks are piled against one another? Look at that ledge that runs along, over there to the right, almost like the rack in a railway-carriage! What accident made that, or was it some forgotten human design?' It looked, indeed, as if it might have been meant for the larder-shelf of some outlaw who had hidden here in days gone by. A piece of white paper – some sandwich-paper, doubtless, that had fallen from above – tried to complete the illusion. 'Yes,' said Bredon, 'you expect to see a notice saying it's for light articles only. By Jove, this is a place!' Forgetting his tremors, he passed by Brinkman, and went exploring further along the gorge. Brinkman followed slowly, almost reluctantly. There was no more conversation till they reached the end of the gorge and climbed up an easy path on to the high road.

Now, surely, if there were going to be any confidential disclosures, they would come. To Bredon's surprise, his companion now seemed to have grown moody and uncommunicative; whatever openings were tried, he not only failed to follow them up, but seemed, by his monosyllabic answers, to be discouraging all approach. Bredon abandoned the effort at last, and returned to the 'Load of Mischief' thoroughly dissatisfied with himself, and more completely mystified than ever.

CHAPTER 15

A Scrap of Paper

LEYLAND met him immediately on his return. He had heard from Angela that Bredon had gone out for a walk with Brinkman, and at Brinkman's invitation, something, too, of the abruptness and the eagerness with which the invitation was issued. Clearly, he was anxious to get first news about Brinkman's disclosures. There was still half an hour or so to waste before luncheon; and Bredon, taking a leaf out of his wife's book, suggested the alehouse bench as a suitable place for talking things over.

'Well?' asked Leyland. 'I never dared to hope that Brinkman would react so quickly. What did he say? Or rather, what can you tell me of what he said?'

'Nothing. Absolutely nothing. He just took me for a walk to the gorge and back.'

'I say, old thing, are you playing quite fair? I mean, if Brinkman only consented to talk to you in confidence, by all means say so, and I'll have to be content.'

'But he didn't. He didn't say a word he mightn't have said in the parlour to all of us. I can't make head or tail of it.'

'Look here, it's absurd trying to palm that off on me. I know you're more scrupulous than I am about these things; but really, what harm can it do to tell me that Brinkman has confided to you? It doesn't make it any easier or any harder for me to put you into the witness-box; and short of that I can't get it out of you if you don't want to tell me. I won't badger you; I won't try and worm it out of you; honestly I won't. But don't pretend that you're still as ignorant of Brinkman's movements this last week as I am.'

'What the devil am I to say? Can't you believe a fellow when he tells the truth? I tell you that all the way to the gorge he talked about anything that came into his head; and coming back from the gorge he wouldn't talk about anything at all – I simply couldn't get him to talk.'

'And *at* the gorge?'

'He talked about the gorge. A regular morning with Herr Baedeker. There really isn't anything more to it.'

'Look here, let's get this straight. We put up a conversation together in a place where we know for a fact that Brinkman's listening behind the wall – and it isn't the first time he's listened to us, either. I explain in a loud voice that I've taken out a warrant, or rather that I'm just going to take out a warrant, for his arrest, and that his best chance of saving himself from arrest is to confide in you or me. An hour or so afterwards he comes up to you, while you're sitting out there with Mrs Bredon in the middle of a conversation. He takes no notice at all of Mrs Bredon, but asks you to come out for a morning walk – on the transparent excuse that he wants to show you this beastly ditch of his. And then he proceeds to waste more than an hour of his time and yours by talking platitudes about the scenery. Are we really going to sit down and admit that?'

'Confound it all; we've got to. I'm no better pleased about it than you are. But God knows I gave him every chance of having a talk if he wanted to.'

'Do you think he was trying to pump you, perhaps? Can't you remember at all what he did talk about?'

'Talked about Pulteney a little. Said he was a typical schoolmaster, or something of that sort. Oh, yes, and he talked about geology – probable age of the earth, if I remember right. Asked me whether I'd been here before. Asked me whether I'd been abroad much. I really can't recall his saying anything else.'

'And you're sure you said nothing which could frighten him, which could put him off?'

'I couldn't have been more careful to avoid it.'

'Well, it's – can you make anything of it yourself?'

'The only idea that occurred to me is that possibly Brinkman wanted me to be away from the house for some reason; and chose this way of making sure that I was.'

'M'm – it's possible, of course. But why should he want you to be away – especially if he's going to be away, too?'

'I know. It doesn't really make sense. I say, Leyland, I'm awfully sorry about this.' He felt absurdly apologetic, though without seeing any way of putting the blame on himself. 'Look here, I'll tell you one thing; it's not in our bargain, of course, but I don't think there's any harm in telling you. Simmonds didn't expect the Euthanasia policy. Or rather, he did expect it to come to him at one time, but not this last week or two, because he'd heard about the codicil leaving it to the Bishop – heard, at any rate, that it wasn't coming to him. So I'm afraid your theory about Simmonds wants revising.'

'It has already been revised. This is very interesting; you say it's certain Simmonds knew about the change of plan?'

'Yes. You can guess the source.'

'And do you suppose he had any idea where the new will was kept? Whether it was up in London, I mean, or in Mottram's own possession?'

'That I couldn't say. Does it make much difference?'

'A lot of difference. Look here, you've been dealing openly with me, so I'll give you some information in return. But I warn you you won't like it, because it doesn't help your theory of suicide a bit. Look here.' He glanced round to see that nobody was watching them, then took an envelope from his pocket, and cautiously shook out on to his open palm a triangle of paper. It was blue, lined paper, with an official sort of look about it. It was obviously a corner left over from a document which had been burned, for the hypotenuse opposite the right angle was a frayed edge of brown ash. The writing on it was 'clerkly' – there is no other word to describe its combination of ugliness with legibility. Only a fragment of writing was left on each of the three lines which the paper contained, for there was a generous allowance of margin. It was a bottom right-hand corner that the fire had spared; and the surviving ends of the lines read as follows:

...queath
...aken out by
...March in the year

'Well, how's that?' said Leyland. 'I don't think we shall differ much over the reading of it.'

'No. It's really rather disappointing, when you are supposed to be a detective, for a document to come to hand in such excellent condition – what there is of it. There aren't two words in the English language that end with the syllable "queath", and unless I am mistaken – no, as you were, the word in the next line might be either "taken" or "mistaken". And of course there's Interlaken, when one comes to think of it, and weaken, and shaken, and oaken, and all sorts of words. But as you say, or rather imply, *taken out by* makes the best sense. And I shall hardly be communicating new impressions to you if I suggest that one speaks of "taking out" insurance policies. Do you happen to know when Mottram took out his Euthanasia? I believe I've got the record upstairs.'

'He took it out in March. There isn't a bit of doubt about this document as it stands. It's the copy of a will, made out by Mottram, having reference to the Euthanasia policy. Now, unless this was a new will altogether – which is possible – that means that this was a copy of his second will, or rather of the codicil which referred to the policy. For in the will, if you remember, there was no allusion to the Euthanasia at all.'

'I suppose it is absolutely certain that this scrap of paper belonged to Mottram?'

'Quite certain – that's the extraordinary thing, the way I found it. The undertaker came round this morning to make ... certain arrangements. As you know, I had taken command of the key of Mottram's room; it's been locked by my orders ever since you and I had that look round – except yesterday, when I took the coroner in. The undertaker came to me for the key this morning, and I went into the room with him; and, just mooning about there aimlessly, I saw something that you and I had failed to see when we were searching the room – this bit of paper. We were not much to blame, for it was rather hidden away, behind the writing-table, that is, between the writing-table and the window. To do us justice, it was under a fold of the table-cloth, but I don't know how we came to overlook it. Considering it was in Mottram's room, I don't think it is a very wild speculation to suppose that it was part of Mottram's will.'

'No, that seems reasonable. And how does it fit into your view of the case? I mean –'

'Oh, of course, it's conceivable that Mottram burned the thing himself. But it doesn't really make very much sense when you come to think of it. We know, and Mottram knew, that it was only a spare copy of the will which the solicitors had got up in London. It wasn't a very important document, therefore, one way or the other. And I'm sure it hasn't escaped your observation, that whereas burning papers is a natural way to get rid of them in winter, when there's a fire in the grate, one doesn't do it in summer unless one's absolutely put to it. Nothing burns more ill-temperedly than a piece of paper when you have to set light to it with a match. You can't even burn it whole, without great difficulty, for you must either keep hold of it, and so leave a corner unburnt, or else leave it lying about in a grate or somewhere, and then the flame generally dies down before it is finished. In this case, it is pretty clear that somebody must have held it in his hand, or it probably wouldn't be a corner that remained unburnt. I can find no finger-marks.'

'Wouldn't a man who was destroying an important document be apt to take care he didn't leave any of it lying about?'

'Certainly, if he'd plenty of time to do it in. If it had been Mottram, for example, burning his own will. It seems to me more like the action of a man in a hurry; and I suspect that the man who burned this document was in a hurry. Or at least he was flustered; for he had been committing a murder, and so few people can keep their heads altogether in that position.'

'It's Simmonds, then, by your way of it?'

'Who else? You see, at first I was in rather a difficulty. We had assumed, what it was natural to assume, that this codicil Mottram added to his will was kept a secret – that Simmonds didn't know about it, and that he'd murdered Mottram under the mistaken idea that he would inherit the Euthanasia benefits as the next of kin. Now, if that had been his intention, it would have been rather a coincidence his *happening* to light on the will and being able to burn it. But you tell me that Simmonds did know about the codicil; very well, that solves the difficulty. It was a double crime not only in fact, but in intention. You thought that Simmonds' knowledge of the codicil gave him a sort of moral alibi. On the contrary, it only fastens the halter round his neck. He determined to destroy Mottram and the will together, and so inherit. The motive is more obvious than ever. The only thing which he unfortunately hadn't taken into account was the fact that the copy of the codicil which he destroyed was a duplicate, and the original was up in London.'

'But isn't it rather a big supposition, that Simmonds not only knew the codicil was in existence, but knew that it was in Mottram's possession when he came down here, and that it would be lying about in Mottram's room, quite easy for him to find?'

'You forget Mottram's psychology. When Simmonds offended him, he wasn't content that Simmonds should be cut out of his will; he wanted him to know that he'd been cut out of the will – directed the lawyers to inform him of the fact. When he added that codicil about the Euthanasia, although he made such a secret of it all round, he was careful, as we know, to inform Simmonds that it had been done. Don't you think it's likely that he wrote to Simmonds and said: "I have willed the Euthanasia policy away to strangers, so as to prevent it coming to you; you can look in on me when I'm at Chilthorpe, and I'll show you the document"? And Simmonds, not understanding the pernicketiness of lawyers, imagined that it would be the original of the will, not a copy, that Mottram had by him. So, when he came round here on his midnight visit, or rather on his early morning visit, he turned off the gas, flung the window open, ransacked the dispatch-box which ·he found lying on the table, found the will, and burnt it hastily at the open window. Probably he thought the unburnt fragment had fallen out of the window; actually it had fallen under the table, and here we are!'

'It was Angela, I suppose, who told you that Simmonds knew he had been cut out of the will?'

'With the best intentions. Mrs Bredon thought, of course, that my suspicion of Simmonds could not survive the revelation. As a matter of fact, it all fitted in nicely. Well, it just shows that one should never waste time trying to puzzle out a problem until one's sure that all the relevant facts have been collated. Here were you and I worrying our lives out over the difficulty, and all because we had never noticed that bit of paper lying on the floor – and might never have noticed it, if I hadn't happened to go in with the undertaker. Now, there's only Brinkman's part of the business to settle. Apart from that, it's as clear as daylight.'

'You think so? Well, you must think me a frightful Sadducee, but even now I don't mind doubling that bet again.'

'Forty pounds! Good Lord, man, the Euthanasia must pay you well! Or do they insure you against losing bets? Well, it would eat a big hole in my salary. But if you want to throw your money away, I don't mind.'

'Good! Forty quid. We'd best keep it dark from Angela, though. I say, when Raight-ho makes that horrible noise on the tom-tom inside, it generally means that Mrs Davis has finished blowing the dust off the cold ham. What's wrong with going in and seeing about a little lunch?'

CHAPTER 16

A Visitor from Pullford

WHEN they came into the coffee-room, Bredon had the instantaneous impression we all get occasionally that the room was too full. Then, on disentangling his sensations, he was delighted to find that the newcomer was Mr Eames, who was exchanging a word or two with Brinkman, though he seemed not to have been introduced to the others. 'Good man!' said Bredon. 'I don't think you met my wife, did you? This is Mr Pulteney ... it was very good of you to keep your promise.'

'As it turned out, I should have had to come in any case. The Bishop had to go off to a Confirmation, so, when he heard the funeral was down here, he sent me to represent him. You see, we heard from the solicitors about our windfall – I suspect you were keeping that dark, Mr Bredon – and he was very much touched by Mr Mottram's kindness. He wished he could have come, Mr Brinkman, but of course a Confirmation is a difficult engagement to get out of.'

'I really knew nothing about the will when I came over to Pullford,' protested Bredon. 'I've heard about it since, of course. Can I offer my congratulations to the diocese, or would it look too much like gifts from the Greeks?'

'Nonsense; you serve your Company, Mr Bredon, and none of us bears you any ill-will for it. I hope, by the way, I have not been indiscreet in mentioning the subject?' he glanced for a moment at the old gentleman. 'The Bishop, of course, has not mentioned the matter except to me, because he quite realizes there may be legal difficulties.'

'I can keep a secret as well as most men,' explained Pulteney. 'That is to say, I have the common human vanity which makes every man like to be in possession of a secret; and perhaps less than my share of the vulgar itch for imparting information. But you know Chilthorpe

113

little, Sir, if you speak of discretion in the same four walls
with Mrs Davis. I assure you that the testamentary dispositions of the late Mr Mottram are seldom off her lips.'

There was a fractional pause, while everybody tried to
think how Mrs Davis knew. Then they remembered that
the matter had been mentioned, though only incidentally,
at the inquest.

'To be sure,' said Eames. 'I have met Mrs Davis before.
If it is true that confession lightens our burdens, the "Load
of Mischief" must sit easily on her.'

'I'm so glad they haven't changed the name of the
inn,' observed Angela. 'These old-fashioned names are
getting so rare. And the "Load of Mischief" is hardly an
encouraging title.'

'There used,' said Eames, 'to be an inn in my old – in
the parish where I lived, which was called "The Labour
in Vain". I sometimes thought of it as an omen.'

'Are you of the funeral party, Mr Pulteney?' asked Leyland, seeing the old gentleman dressed in deep black.

'There is no hiding anything from you detectives. Yes,
I have promised myself the rustic treat of a funeral. In the
scholastic profession such thrills are rare; they make us
retire at sixty nowadays. My lot is cast amidst the young;
I see ever fresh generations succeeding to the old, filling
up the gaps in the ranks of humanity; and I confess that
when one sees the specimens one sometimes doubts
whether the process is worth while. But do not let me cast
a gloom over our convivialities. Let us eat and drink,
Mrs Davis's shape seems to say to us, for tomorrow we die.'

'I hope I oughtn't to have gone,' said Angela. 'I'd
have brought my blacks if I'd thought of it.'

'Without them, you would be a glaring offence against
village etiquette. No, Mrs Bredon, your presence would
not be expected. The Company needs no representatives
at the funeral; more practical, it sheds golden tears over
the coffin. For the rest of us it is different. Mr Eames pays
a last tribute to his diocesan benefactor. Mr Brinkman,
like a good secretary, must dispatch the material envelope
to its permanent address. For myself, what am I? A fellow-
wayfarer in an inn; and yet what more is any of us, in this
brief world? No, Mrs Bredon, you are exempt.'

'Oh, do stop him,' said Angela. 'How did you come down, Mr Eames?'

'By the midday train, a funereal pageant in itself. Was Mr Mottram much known in the neighbourhood?'

'He is now,' replied Mr Pulteney, with irrepressible ghoulishness. 'The victim of sudden death is like a diver; no instinct of decency withholds us from watching his taking-off.'

'I don't think he had any near relations living,' said Brinkman, 'except young Simmonds. He'll be there, I suppose; but there wasn't much love lost between them. He will hardly be interested, anyhow, in the reading of the will.'

'By the way, Mr Brinkman, his Lordship asked me to say that you will be very welcome at Cathedral House, if you are detained in Pullford at all.'

'It is extremely kind of him. But I had wound up all Mr Mottram's outstanding affairs before he came away for his holiday, and I don't suppose I shall be needed. I was thinking of going up to London in a day or two. I have to shift for myself, you see.'

'Have some coffee, Eames,' suggested Bredon; 'you must need it after a tiring journey like that.'

'Thanks, I think I will. Not that I'm tired, really. It makes so much difference on the railway if you are occupied.'

'You don't mean to say you are one of those fortunate creatures who can *work* in railway trains?'

'No, not work. I played patience all the way.'

'Patience? Did I hear you say patience? Ah, but you only brought one pack, of course.'

'No, I always travel with two.'

'Two? And Mr Pulteney has two! Angela, that settles it! This afternoon I shall have a game.'

'Miles, dear, not *the* game? You know you can't play that and think of anything else at the same time. Mr Eames, would you mind dropping your packs in the river? You see, it's so bad for my husband; he sits down to an interminable game of patience, and forgets all about his work and everything.'

'You don't understand, Angela; it clears the brain.

When you've been puzzled over a thing, as I have been over this question of suicide, your brains get all stale and used up, and you must give them a fresh start. A game of patience will just do the trick. No, no milk, thanks. Would you tell Mrs Davis' – this was to the barmaid – 'that I shall be very busy all the latter part of this afternoon, and mustn't be disturbed on any account? It's all right, Angela; I'll give you half an hour now to remonstrate with me, but it won't be any use.'

It was not, as a matter of fact, till after the funeral party had left, and the coffin been removed, that Miles and Angela forgathered. They went to the old mill-house, feeling that it would be a safe place for confidences now that Brinkman was otherwise engaged. 'Well,' said Angela, 'I suppose you're wanting some Watson-work?'

'Badly. Look here, one of us, either Leyland or I, is beginning to feel the strain a bit. Everything that crops up makes him more and more determined to have Simmonds' blood, and me more and more inclined to stick to my old solution.'

'You haven't been doubling that bet again, have you?'

'That's a detail. Look here, I must tell you all about his find this morning.' And he proceeded to explain the whole business of the piece of paper, and Leyland's inferences from it. 'Now,' he finished up, 'what d'you make of all that?'

'Well, he has got a case, hasn't he? I mean, his explanation would explain things.'

'Yes, but look at the difficulties.'

'Let's have them. No, wait a minute, I believe I can do the difficulties. Let's try a little womanly intuish. First – you'd have noticed the piece of paper if it had been there when you went in.'

'Not necessarily. It's wonderful what one can overlook if one isn't thinking about it.'

'Well, then, Simmonds wouldn't have been such a chump as to burn the thing on the spot. Especially with a foul smell of gas in the room, not to mention the corpse. He'd have shoved it into his pocket and taken it home.'

'There's a good deal in that. But Leyland would say that Simmonds was afraid to do that for fear he should be

116

stopped and searched.'

'Pretty thin. And then, of course, if it was really important for him to get the document out of the way, he wouldn't have left a bit lying about. He'd have seen that it was *all* burnt.'

'Leyland says that was because he was in a hurry.'

'Well, let's have some others. I'm used up.'

'Well, don't you see that a man who is burning an important document, holding it in his hand all the time, takes it up by the least important corner, probably a blank space at the top? This is the work of a man who wasn't particularly keen on destroying all traces of the document, and he held it by the bottom right hand corner, as one naturally would.'

'Why not the left hand, and the match in one's right? Ha! The left-handed criminal. We *are* in luck.'

'Don't you believe it. You start holding it at the left hand corner, and then transfer it to your right hand when you've thrown the match away. You try, next time you're burning your dressmaker's bill. And here's another point. Simmonds would have been bound to stand with his head right in the window, to keep clear of the gas fumes. Almost certainly he would have put the paper down on the window-sill and let it burn, leaving one of those curious damp marks. He didn't, because I should have been bound to notice that; I was looking for marks on the window-sill. If he held it in his hand, he would be holding it outside the window, and he wouldn't be such a chump as to throw away the odd corner in the room, when he could pitch it out of the window. Another thing, he wouldn't have dared to burn a light at the window like that, for fear of attracting attention.'

'Well, I still think my objections were more important. But go on.'

'Well, since that piece of paper wasn't dropped in the room before Leyland and I went into it, probably not, anyhow, it looks as if it had been dropped in the room since Leyland and I went into it. Or at any rate, since the first police search. Because the room has been kept locked, one way and another, since then.'

'There was no deceiving this man.'

117

'Which makes it very improbable that the piece of paper was dropped there by accident at all. Anybody who went in there had no business to go in there and would be jolly careful not to leave any traces. We are therefore irresistibly compelled, my dear Angela, to the conclusion that somebody dropped it there on purpose.'

'That firm grasp of the obvious. Yes?'

'He put it there deliberately, to create an impression. Now, it might be to create the impression that Simmonds was the murderer. To whose advantage would that be?'

'Mr Leyland's.'

'Angela, don't be flippant. Is there anybody?'

'Well, Mr Simmonds hasn't any enemies that we know of. Unless it was somebody who was disappointed in the quality of his handkerchiefs. What you *want* me to say is, that it must be somebody who has murdered Mottram himself, and wants to save his skin by pretending it was Simmonds as did it.'

'I'm dashed if I want you to say that. In fact, it's just what I didn't want you to say. Of course, if you assume that Mottram was murdered by Brinkman, it does all work out, most unpleasantly well. You see, when Leyland and I were sitting here, talking *at* Brinkman, who was hiding behind the wall, Leyland did say that the only thing which prevented him from arresting Simmonds was the fact that he'd no evidence to connect him with the actual room. I could see what he was up to – he wanted Brinkman to take the hint (assuming, of course, that he was the real murderer) and start manufacturing clues to incriminate Simmonds. Well, it looks very much as if Brinkman had taken the hint, and was doing identically what Leyland suggested. Curse it all.'

'Still, it was clever of Brinky to get in when the door was locked.'

'Oh, that's nothing. I wouldn't put it beyond Brinkman to have a duplicate key of that door. No, I've nothing to fall back on really except the absence of motive. What earthly reason had Brinkman for wanting to do Mottram in? Or rather, I have one other thing to fall back on. But it's not evidence; it's instinct.'

'As how?'

'Why, don't you see that the whole thing works out too beastly well? Isn't it rather too obviously a ruse? I mean, that idea of dropping a piece of paper with only half a dozen words on it, and yet those half-dozen words showing exactly what the document was? Isn't it rather too obviously a plant?'

'But it was a plant, if Brinky put it there.'

'Yes, but isn't it *too* obviously a plant? So obviously, I mean, that you couldn't expect anybody, even Leyland, to think for a moment that it was genuine? Can Brinkman really have thought that Leyland wouldn't see through it?'

'But if he didn't think so –'

'Double bluff, my good woman, double bluff. I can tell you, crime is becoming quite a specialized profession nowadays. Don't you see that Brinkman argued to himself like this: "If I leave an obviously faked clue lying about like this, Leyland will immediately think that it is a faked clue, used by one criminal to shove off the blame on another. Who the criminals are, or which is which, doesn't matter. It will convince him that there has, after all, been a murder. And it will disguise from him the fact that it was suicide." Of course, all that's making Brinkman out to be a pretty smart lad. But I fancy he is a pretty smart lad. And I read that piece of paper as a bit of double bluff, meant to harden the ingenious Leyland in his belief that the suicide was a murder.'

'Ye-es. It'll look pretty thin before a jury, won't it?'

'Don't I know that it'll look thin before a jury? Especially as, on my showing, Brinkman was prepared to let suspicion of murder rest on himself rather than admit it was suicide. But what beats me is the motive. There's no doubt that Brinkman is a fanatical anti-clerical, and would do anything to prevent Mottram's money going to a Catholic diocese... I say, what's that?'

A sudden sneeze, an unmistakable sneeze, had come from somewhere immediately behind them. In a twinkling Bredon had rushed round to the other side of the wall. But there was nobody there.

CHAPTER 17

Mysterious Behaviour of the Old Gentleman

BREDON and his wife looked at one another in astonish-
ment. It was impossible than the funeral should yet be
over; impossible, surely, that Brinkman, whose place in
the pageant was such a prominent one, should have
absented himself from the ceremony unnoticed. There
was no doubt as to the path which the self-betrayed listener must have taken. From behind the wall, there was a
gap in a privet-hedge, and through this there was a direct
and speedy retreat to the back-door of the inn. The inn
itself, when they went back to it, was as silent as the grave
– indeed, the comparison forced itself upon their minds.
It was as if the coffin from upstairs had taken all human
life away with it, when it went on its last journey, leaving
nothing but the ticking of clocks and the steaming of a
kettle in the kitchen to rob solitude of its silence. Outside,
the sun still shone brightly, though there was a menacing
bank of cloud coming up, now, from the south. The air
felt breathless and oppressive; not a door could bang, not
a window rattle. The very flies on the window-panes
seemed drowsy. They passed from room to room, in the
vain hope of discovering an intruder; everywhere the
same loneliness, the same stillness met them. Bredon had
an odd feeling as if they ought, after all, to be at the
funeral; it was so like the emptiness of his old school when
everybody was out of doors except himself, one summer
day.

'I can't stand much of this,' he said. 'Let's go down
towards the churchyard, and see if we can meet them
coming back. Then at least we shall be in a position to
know who *wasn't* there.'

The expedition, however, proved abortive; they met
Eames almost on the doorstep, and down the street
figures melting away by twos and threes from the churchyard showed that the funeral was at an end. 'I say, come
in here,' said Bredon. 'I want to talk things over a bit, Mr

120

Eames.' And the three retired into that 'best room' where tea had been laid on the afternoon of Bredon's arrival. 'You've just come back from the funeral?'

'This moment. Why?'

'Can you tell us for certain who was there? Was Brinkman there, for example?'

'Certainly. He was standing just next me.'

'And Mr Simmonds from the shop – do you know him by sight?'

'He was pointed out to me as the chief mourner. I had a word with him afterwards. But why all this excitement about the local celebrities?'

'Tell him, Miles,' said Angela. 'He may be able to throw some light on all this.' And Bredon told Eames of the strange eavesdropping that went on behind the mill-house wall; something, too, of the suspicions which he and Leyland entertained, and the difficulty they both found in giving any explanation of the whole tragedy.

'Well, it's very extraordinary. Pulteney, of course, didn't go after all –'

'Pulteney didn't go?'

'No; didn't you hear him say, soon after luncheon, that his good resolutions had broken down, and that he wasn't going to the funeral after all? I thought it rather extraordinary at the time.'

'You mean his sudden change of plan?'

'No, the reason he gave for it. He said the afternoon was too tempting, and he really must go out fishing.'

'Is that a very odd reason for Pulteney? He's an incalculable sort of creature.'

'Yes, but it doesn't happen to be true. Can't you feel the thunder in the air? If you can't, the fishes can. And when there's thunder in the air they won't rise. Pulteney knows that as well as I do.'

'Would you know his rod if you saw it?'

'Yes, I was looking at it with him just before luncheon.'

'Come on.' They went out into the front hall, and Eames gave a quick glance round. 'Yes, that's it, in the corner. He's no more out fishing than you or I.'

'Edward!' said Angela as they returned to the best room. 'To think it was my Edward all the time.'

'Oh, don't rag, Angela; this is serious. Now, can it have been Pulteney listening all along?'

'He was there, you know, when you and Leyland arranged to go out to the mill-house after breakfast. And he was there at luncheon, though I don't think either of us mentioned that we meant to go there. Still, he might have guessed that. But what on earth is the poor old dear up to?'

'Well, one or two things are clear. About Brinkman, I mean. Whatever his idea may have been when he took me out for a walk to the gorge and talked about geology, he wasn't "reacting" on Leyland's suggestion, because it wasn't he who was listening behind the wall when the suggestion was made. And there's another thing – this bit of paper Leyland found lying about in the room upstairs. If Brinkman put it there, then Brinkman did it on his own; he wasn't playing up to the suggestion which Leyland made about wanting clues to incriminate Simmonds with.'

'Still,' objected Angela, 'we never proved that it *was* Brinky who left that old clue lying about. We only assumed it, because we thought it was Brinky who was listening behind the wall.'

'You mean that if Pulteney was listening, and Pulteney was – well, was somehow interested in confusing the tracks of the murder, it may have been he who left the bit of paper under the table.'

'I didn't say so. But it seems quite as much on the cards as anything else in this frightful business.'

'Let's see, now, what do we know about Pulteney? We know, in the first place, that he was sleeping in the house on the night when Mottram died. Actually, he had the room next door to Mottram's – between his and the one we've got now. According to his own evidence, he slept soundly all night, and heard nothing. On the other hand, his own evidence showed that he went to bed after Mottram and Brinkman, and we've nothing, therefore, to confirm his own account of his movements. He was woken up the next morning after the tragedy had occurred, and when he was told about it all he said was – what was it, Angela?'

'*In that case, Mrs Davis, I shall fish the Long Pool this morning.*'

'That might almost be represented as suggesting that he wasn't exactly surprised when he heard of Mottram's death, mightn't it? All his references to Mottram's death since then have been rather – shall we say? – lacking in feeling. He, no less than Brinkman, seemed to be anxious that we should interpret the death as suicide, because it was he who suggested to me that idea about Mottram having brought down the wrong flies, as if he never really had any intention of fishing at all. He has been rather inquisitive about when Brinkman was leaving, and when we were leaving, too, for that matter. That's all you can scrape together, I think, against his general behaviour. And against that, of course, you've got to put the absence of all known motive.'

'And the general character of the man,' suggested Eames.

'I suppose so. ... What impression exactly does he make on you?'

'Why, that he is out of touch with real life. All that *macabre* humour of his about corpses and so on is an academic thing – he has never really felt death close to. I don't say that a superb actor mightn't adopt that ironical pose. I only say it's far more natural to regard him as a harmless old gentleman, who reflects and doesn't act. It's very seldom that you find the capacity for acute reflection and the capacity for successful action combined in the same character. At least, that's always been my impression.'

'Well, granted that we acquit him of the main charge, as Leyland would acquit Brinkman of the main charge, he still comes under the minor suspicion of eavesdropping. He's as good a candidate for that position as Brinkman himself, only that it was Brinkman's brand of cigarette we found behind the wall yesterday.'

'Edward had run out, you remember,' suggested Angela. 'He might have borrowed one from Brinky, or pinched it when he wasn't looking. And, to be accurate, we must remember that the first time we were overheard, when we were talking in my room, the listener had disappeared before you got into the passage, and the next room to ours is Edward's.'

123

'And besides, we know now that it wasn't Brinkman, this time at any rate. Because he was away at the funeral. Whereas Pulteney shirked the funeral on an obviously false ground; didn't go to the funeral and didn't go fishing either. Assuming that the listener is the same all through, it looks bad for Pulteney.'

A knock at the door suddenly interrupted their interview. 'May I come in?' said a gentle voice, and following it, flushed as with hot walking, yet still beaming with its habitual benevolence, came the face of Mr Pulteney.

'Ah, Mr Bredon, they told me I would find you in here. I wanted a word with you. Could we go outside, or –'

'Nonsense, Mr Pulteney,' said Angela firmly. 'What Mr Eames and I don't know isn't worth knowing. Come in and tell us all about it.'

'Well, you know, I'm afraid I've got to make a kind of confession. It's a very humiliating confession for me to make, because I'm afraid, once again, I've been guilty of curiosity. I simply cannot mind my own business.'

'And what have you been up to now?' asked Angela.

'Why, when I said I was going out fishing this afternoon, I'm afraid I was guilty of a prevarication. Indeed, when I announced my intention of going to the funeral, I was beginning to weave the tangled web of those who first practise to deceive. You see, I didn't want Brinkman to know.'

'To know what?'

'Well, that I was rather suspicious about his movements. You see, I've asked him several times when he means to leave Chilthorpe, and he always talks as if he was quite uncertain of his plans. He did so at breakfast, you remember. But this morning, when I went up to get a sponge I had left in the bathroom, I saw Brinkman packing.'

'Packing?'

'Well, he was wandering about the room clearing up his papers, and there was a dispatch-box open on the table, and a suit-case on the floor. And, as I knew he was due to be at the funeral, I thought this was rather a funny time for him to want to leave. Especially as he'd given no notice to Mrs Davis. So I wondered whether, perhaps, there was anything behind it.'

'You did well to wonder,' said Bredon. 'So what did you do?'

'Well, it stuck in my head that Mottram, when he came down here, came in a motor-car. Mrs Davis, though her trade announcement advertises good accommodation for man and beast, does not run to a garage. There is only one in Chilthorpe; you can just see it down the road there. Now, thought I, if by any chance Mr Brinkman is meditating a precipitate disappearance, it would be like his caution to have made all arrangements beforehand. And if I went down to the garage and had a look at the car, it might be that I, though heaven knows I am no motorist, should be able to see whether he had got the car in proper trim for a journey.'

'You must have talked very nicely to the garage people,' suggested Angela. 'It would never do if you were suspected of being a motor-thief.'

'Well, I had to do my best. I changed my mind about going to the funeral, and made the excuse that I wanted to go fishing. I heard you gasp, Mr Eames; but Brinkman knows nothing about fishing. Then, when you had started, I went off to the garage by myself. Fortunately, very fortunately for my purpose, it proved that there was nobody in. There are only two men, in any case, and they neglect their business a good deal. I had an excuse if one was needed, but when I found myself alone in the garage I flung caution to the winds. There was a card-case inside which showed me which Mottram's car was. My investigations led me to the conclusion that the car was in readiness for an immediate and secret departure for some considerable journey.'

'Do tell us what they were,' said Angela demurely. 'Just for the interest of the thing.'

'Well, I removed with some difficulty a kind of cap from that thing behind, which put me in a position to examine the interior of what is, I suspect, called the petrol-tank. The careful insertion of a pencil showed that the tank was quite full; which suggested that a refill had been obtained since they arrived.'

'They might have run short on the journey down, a mile or two out,' suggested Angela. 'But this was not all?'

'No, there was a map lying on the driver's seat, somewhat carelessly folded up. I thought it a point of interest that this map did not include Pullford, and seemed to contemplate an expedition to the west or south-west.'

'There's not a great deal in that,' said Bredon. 'Still, it's suggestive. Anything else?'

'Well, you know, I lifted up one of the seats, and found there a collection of sandwiches and a large flask of whisky.'

'The devil you did! But they might have been for the journey down here. Did you taste the sandwiches to see if they were fresh?'

'I took that liberty. They seemed to me, I must say, a trifle on the stale side. But who was I to complain? I was, as it were, a guest. Meanwhile, let me point out to you the improbability of Mottram's loading up his car with sandwiches for a twenty–mile drive.'

'That's true. Were they properly cut? Professional work, I mean?'

'I suspected the hand of the artist. Mrs Davis, no doubt. The whisky I did not feel at liberty to broach. But the idea suggested itself to me that these were the preparations of a man who is contemplating a considerable journey, and probably one which will not allow him time to take his meals at a public-house.'

'And why a secret departure?'

'Why, somebody had induced a coat of black paint over what I take to be the number-plate of the car. I am a mere novice in such matters, but is that usual?'

'It is not frequently done. And was the paint still wet?'

'That is a curious point. The paint was dry. I supposed, then, that Brinkman's preparations for departure were not made yesterday or the day before.'

'It's awfully kind of you to take all this trouble, and to come and tell us.'

'Not at all. I thought perhaps it might be worth mentioning, in case you thought it best, well, to lay hands, somehow, on Brinkman.'

'Why, Mr Pulteney,' said Angela, bubbling over, 'we were just preparing to lay hands on you!'

CHAPTER 18

The Barmaid is Brought to Book

THE bewilderment registered by Mr Pulteney's face at this extraordinary announcement rapidly gave way to a look of intense gratification. 'At last,' he said, 'I have lived! To be mistaken for a criminal, perhaps a murderer – it is my *Nunc Dimittis*. All these years I have lived the blameless life of one who is continually called upon to edify his juniors; I have risen early, in order to convict my pupils of the sin of being late; I have eaten sparingly, in order to pretend that the food provided by our establishment is satisfying when it is not; I have pretended to sentiments of patriotism, of rugged sportsmanship, of moral approval or indignation, which I did not feel. There is little to choose, believe me, between the fakir and the schoolmaster; either must spend days of wearisome mortification, because that is the way in which he gets his living. And now, for one crowded hour of glorious old age, I have been mistaken for a guilty intriguer. The blood flows richer in my veins; I am overcome with gratitude. If only I could have kept it up!'

'Mr Eames,' said Angela, 'there's one thing you said which you've got to take back. You said Mr Pulteney was too much a man of reflection to be a man of action as well. And now you've heard how he broke into a garage, stole a piece of sandwich, and took the cap off a petrol-tank without being in the least certain that the car wouldn't explode. Is this the pale scholar you pictured to us?'

'I apologize,' said Eames. 'I apologize to Mr Pulteney unreservedly. I will form no more judgements of character. You may tell me that Mrs Davis is a murderess, if you will, and I will discuss the proposition on its merits.'

'Talking of which,' said Angela, 'the cream of the situation is that we *still* don't know who it was that was rubbering behind that beastly mill-house.'

'Oh, as to that,' said Eames diffidently, 'I've felt fairly

certain about that all along. I suppose it's the result of living with priests that one becomes thus worldly-wise. But didn't you know, Mr Bredon, that maids always steal their masters' cigarettes? It is, I believe, a more or less recognized form of perquisite. Every liberty taken by the rich is aped by their domestics. And, although she is not in household service, I have no doubt that the barmaid here claims a like privilege.'

'Do you mean –' began Bredon.

'You noticed, surely, that her fingers are a little stained with brown? I noticed it when she brought in my fried eggs. Ladies generally have expensive tastes in cigarettes, and I have no doubt that this maid would go for the "Callipoli" if she got a chance.'

'Miles, dear,' said Angela softly, 'who was it said that it must be a servant who was listening at our bedroom door?'

'The uneducated do not take Mr Pulteney's view about curiosity. I daresay this young lady often listens at keyholes. With a corpse in the house, and detectives about, she listens with all the more avidity. And if the detectives insist on exchanging confidences close to that precise point in the shrubbery at which she is in the habit of smoking purloined cigarettes, they put themselves in her hands. But a stronger motive supervenes; what she overhears out of pure curiosity turns out to be of vital importance to herself. She learns that the young man she is walking out with is suspected of murder.'

'Good Lord, and of course it was she who reacted on our suggestions, not Brinkman! I don't know if I mentioned it to you, Angela, but when Leyland and I were talking together at the mill-house, he said the only thing that would make him hesitate to arrest Simmonds would be evidence showing that Simmonds knew he wasn't Mottram's heir. And it was exactly that evidence which Raightho proceeded to produce.'

'Oh,' cried Angela, 'how perfectly odious! You mean that when I thought I was pumping Emmeline so cleverly, and getting out of her exactly what I wanted, she was really doing it all on purpose, and telling me exactly what *she* wanted?'

'I'm afraid so, my dear. A lot of reputations seem to be going west today. And, of course, I should say it's odds that her whole story was absolutely trumped up, invented to suit the occasion. And we're back exactly where we were, not knowing whether Simmonds knew he was cut out of the will or not.'

'On the other hand,' said Angela, 'we do know, now, what put the wind up young Simmonds so badly. When you and Leyland passed him and Emmeline in the lane last night, she was telling him that he was suspected of murder, and had better be dashed careful what he said and who he said it to. Naturally, it gave him a bit of a fright when he thought you were going to pump him about his uncle.'

'And meanwhile, what has Brinkman been up to? We've really no evidence against him until all this about the car cropped up. Dash it all, and just when I was going to get a game of patience!'

'I don't want to put my oar in unduly,' said the old gentleman in an apologetic tone, 'but might it not be a good thing to acquaint Mr Leyland with the somewhat unusual state of affairs down at the garage? If Brinkman really intends to do what is popularly known as a bunk, he may be off at any moment. Had I been more expert, I could no doubt have immobilized some important part of the mechanism. As it was, I was helpless.'

'Where is Leyland, by the way?' asked Bredon.

'He is just coming up the street now,' said Eames, looking out of the window. 'I'll call to him to come in here.'

'Hullo, what have you been up to?' asked Bredon, as Leyland entered.

'Why, to tell the truth, I have been shadowing Mr Pulteney. I must apologize, Mr Pulteney, but I felt bound to be careful. I've had you kept under close observation all this week; and it was only as I stood behind the door, watching your investigations into that car, that I became perfectly convinced of your innocence.'

'What! More suspicion! This is indeed a day. Why, if I had had the least conception that you were watching me, Mr Leyland, I would have led you a rare dance! My movements, I promise you, should have been full of mystery. I should have gone out every night with a scowl and a dark lantern. I am overwhelmed.'

'Well, I must apologize at least for spying upon your detective work. You do very well for an amateur, Mr Pulteney, but you are not suspicious enough.'

'Indeed! I overlooked something? How mortifying!'

'Yes, when you took the cushion off that front seat, you failed to observe that there was a neat tear in it, which had been quite recently sewn up. Otherwise I am sure that you would have done what I did just now – cut it open.'

'And is it fair to ask what you found inside?'

'Well, we seem to have gone too far now to have any secrets between us. I feel sure that both you, Mr Pulteney, and you, Mr Eames, are anxious to see justice done, and are prepared to help at least by your silence.'

'To be sure,' said Pulteney.

'I am at your service,' said Eames.

'Well, this is actually what I found.' With a dramatic gesture he produced a small waterproof wallet, and turned out its contents. 'You will find a thousand pounds there, all in Bank of England notes.'

'Well,' said Bredon, when the exclamations of surprise had died away, 'are you still suspecting young Simmonds?'

'I'm not easy about him yet in my own mind. But of course, I see Brinkman's deeper in this business than I had suspected so far. A man who's innocent doesn't prepare to do a bolt with a thousand pounds and a motor-car that doesn't belong to him.'

'Well,' said Bredon, 'I suppose we ought to be keeping an eye on Mr Brinkman.'

'My dear old thing,' said Leyland, 'don't you realize that I've had two of my men at the "Swan" all this week, and that Brinkman hasn't been unaccounted for for one moment? The trouble is, he knows he's being watched, so he won't give himself away. At least, I'm pretty sure of it. But the motor, of course, puts us in a very good position. We know how he means to escape, and we can afford to take the watch off him and put it on the motor instead. Then he'll show his hand, because he's mad keen to be off. At present he's in his room, smoking a cigarette and

reading an old novel. He won't move, I think, until he
makes certain that we're all out of the way. Probably not
till after supper, because a night ride will suit his purpose
best. And he's got a night for it, too; there's a big storm
coming on, unless I'm mistaken.'

'And what about Simmonds?' asked Bredon.

'And the barmaid?' added Angela.

'Well, of course I could question both or either of them.
But I'd sooner not, if I can help it; it's cruel work. I was
wondering if you, Mrs Bredon, could go and have a talk
to that maid after we've had our tea, and see what satisfaction you can get out of her?'

'I don't mind at all. In fact, I rather want to have it
out with dear Emmeline. I owe her one, you see. Meanwhile, let's have tea by all means. I wonder if Brinky will
come down to it?'

Brinkman did come down, and tea was not a very en-
livening meal. Everybody in the room looked upon him
as a man who was probably a murderer and certainly a
thief. Consequently everybody tried to be nice to him,
and everybody's style was cramped by the effort. Even
Mr Pulteney's verbosity seemed to have been dried up by
the embarrassment of the situation. On the whole, Eames
carried it off best. His dry, melancholy manner was quite
unaltered; he talked about patience to Bredon, he talked
Pullford gossip to Brinkman; he tried to draw out Pulteney
on educational questions. But most of the party were glad
when it was over, when Brinkman had shut himself up
again, and Angela had betaken herself to the back premises to have it out with the barmaid.

The 'best room' had been turned by common consent
into a sort of committee-room; during all this whirligig of
sensations, the background of their mind was filled with
those protuberant portraits of the late Mr Davis which so
defiantly occupied the walls. It was here that Angela found
them assembled when she came up, some half an hour
later, a little red about the eyes.

'Well, I didn't try any subterfuges this time; I let her
have it straight from the shoulder. And then she cried,
and I cried, and we both cried together a good bit.'

'The mysterious sex again,' said Mr Pulteney.

'Oh, you wouldn't understand, of course. Anyhow, she's had a rotten time. That first evening, when she listened outside the door, it was only for a moment or two, out of sheer curiosity, and she didn't hear anything that interested her. It was yesterday evening, when you two were talking, that she got interested. She overheard at first merely by accident, which just shows how careful you ought to be. She caught the name "Simmonds"; she heard, for the first time, about the Euthanasia policy, and what it might have meant to him and to her. She went on listening, naturally, and so she came in for all Mr Ley-land's exposition of the case against Simmonds. You didn't convince my husband, Mr Leyland, but you had a much greater success on the other side of the wall. The poor girl, who's been brought up on novelettes and penny shockers all her life, drank in the whole story. She really believed that the man who had been making love to her, the man she was in love with, was a cold-blooded murderer. She acted, I think, very well. He came round that evening to take her out for an evening walk, and on the way she taxed him with his supposed crime. If you come to think of it, that was sporting of her.'

'It was,' said Leyland. 'People are found dead in ditches for less than that.'

'Well, anyhow, it worked all right. Simmonds listened to her charges, and then denied them all. He didn't give her any evidence for his denial much, but she believed him. There was no quarrel. Next day, that is to say this morning, Emmeline heard you two arranging for a talk at the mill-house. She didn't suspect the trap; she walked straight into it. What she heard made her believe that there was only one way to save Simmonds – to pretend that he knew about the Euthanasia, and knew the money wasn't coming to him. The poor girl reflected that Simmonds had been hanging round the house on the night of Mottram's death; he had been there waiting to see her, when she left the bar at closing time. So, bravely again, I think, she came to me with her story about the anonymous friend and her young man with his lost legacy. Of course, by sheer accident I made it much easier for her to pitch me this yarn, and I swallowed it whole. She thought that, with some blackening of her own conscience, she had saved an innocent man's life.'

'And that's all she knows, so far?'

'No; at the end of lunch she heard you, Miles, saying that you'd give me half an hour to talk things over. So when she saw us stealing down to the now familiar trysting-place by the mill – she hadn't gone to the funeral – she followed us and listened again. And, to her horror, she realized from what you said that all her lying had failed to do its work. Leyland still believed, believed more than ever, that her young man was the criminal. Her anxiety put her off her guard, and a sudden sneeze gave her away. She didn't dare to go back to the house; she hid in the privet-hedge.'

'And the long and short of it is,' suggested Leyland, 'that her story is no evidence at all. Simmonds may be as guilty or as innocent as you like; she knew nothing about it. Can she give any account of Simmonds' movements on the night of the murder?'

'Well, she says she had to be in the bar up to closing-time, and then she slipped round to the back door, where he was waiting for her, and stood there talking to him.'

'For how long?'

'She says it might have been a quarter of an hour, or it might have been three-quarters of an hour; she really couldn't say.'

'That sounds pretty thin.'

'How impossible you bachelors are! Miles, can't you explain to him? Oh, well, I suppose it's no use; you couldn't possibly understand.'

'It's certainly rather an unfortunate circumstance for Simmonds that, just at the moment the gas was turned on in Mottram's room, he was indulging in a kind of ecstasy which may have lasted a quarter of an hour; or may have lasted three-quarters.'

'Meanwhile,' said Bredon, 'I hope you realize that your own case against Simmonds is considerably weaken-ed? You were trying to make out, if you remember, that Simmonds murdered Mottram and burned the will, knowing that the will cut him out of his inheritance. But since we have learned to discredit the testimony of Raight-

ho, we have no evidence that Simmonds ever knew anything about the will, or had ever so much as heard of the
Euthanasia policy.'

'That's true. And it's also true that these last discoveries
have made me more inclined to suspect Brinkman. I shall
have to keep my eye on Simmonds, but for the time being
Brinkman is the quarry we must hunt. It's Brinkman's
confession I look forward to for the prospect of those forty
pounds.'

'Well, if you can catch Brinkman and make him confess, you're welcome to them. Or even if Brinkman does
himself in somehow, commits suicide rather than face the
question, I'll give you the benefit of the doubt, and we'll
treat it as murder. Meanwhile, if you will excuse me, I
think, I've just time to lay out that patience before
supper.'

'Oh, he's hopeless,' said Angela.

CHAPTER 19

How Leyland Spent the Evening

BREDON was not allowed to escape so easily. Leyland
insisted that their plans must be settled at once, before
supper-time. 'You see,' he said, 'we've got to make rings
round Brinkman, and he's got to fancy that he is not under
observation. That's going to be a difficult job. But it's
made easy for us, rather, by the fact that Friday night
is cinema night in Chilthorpe.'

'A cinema at Chilthorpe!' protested Mr Pulteney.
'Good God!'

'Yes, there's a sort of barn out behind the Rectory, and
one of these travelling shows comes round once a week or
once a fortnight. It's extraordinary how civilization has
developed, isn't it? My idea was this; our friend the barmaid is to come in at supper, and ask us if we shall be
wanting anything for the night, and whether she can go
out. The Boots, she will say quite truthfully, is going to the
cinema, and she wants to do the same. Mrs Davis will be
kept busy at the bar. Therefore there will be nobody to
attend to the bell if we ring – she will ask us whether we
mind that.'

'Machiavellian,' said Mr Pulteney.

'Then somebody – you, Mrs Bredon, for choice – will
suggest *our* making up a party for the cinema. Your husband will refuse, because he wants to stay at home playing
patience.'

'Come, I like this scheme,' said Bredon. 'It seems to me
to be all on the right lines. I only hope that you will allow
me to be as good as my word.'

'That's all right; I'm coming to that. The rest of us
will consent to accompany Mrs Bredon; Brinkman, presumably, will refuse. Soon after supper – the performance
is at eight – we will all leave the house in the direction of
the cinema, which is fortunately the opposite direction
from the garage.'

'And have I got to sit through an evening performance

135

in the barn?' asked Angela.

'Why, no. I want you and Mr Eames to make your way back to the inn, by turning off along the lane which leads to the old mill; then you can come in quietly by the privet-hedge at the back. Then I want you, Mr Eames, to wait about in the passage which leads to the bar, dodging down the cellar stairs if Brinkman comes to the bar to have a fortifier on his way. I hope your reputation will not suffer from these movements. You will keep your eye on the front of the house, in case Brinkman goes out that way.'

'He's a fool if he does,' said Bredon. 'In the first place, it's a shorter way to the garage to take the path that goes out at the back. And in the second place, if he takes that path, he will be unnoticed, whereas if he comes out by the front-door he will be under the eyes of the bar-parlour.'

'I know, and I am going to discourage him still further from going out at the front by leaving you to keep a look out. Your window faces the front, doesn't it? Very well, then, you will sit in your room playing patience, but right in the window-seat, please, and with the blind up.'

'But I say, if he goes by the front way, have I got to track him? Because –'

'No, you haven't. Mr Eames is to do that. You sit still where you are and go on playing patience. Mr Eames, if Brinkman goes out by the front-door, you will see him; you will wait till he is round the corner, and then follow him at a distance. That, of course, is only to make sure what he does on the way to the garage; you are not to overtake him or interfere with him.'

'I see.'

'And what am I to do?' asked Angela.

'Well, I was wondering if, on returning from our false start, you would mind going up unnoticed to your husband's room? The back-stairs are very handy for the purpose. You could sit there reading, or anything, and then if Brinkman does leave by the front, your husband, while still sitting at the window and pretending not to notice, could pass the word to you. You would then go downstairs and ring up the garage, so that we shall be ready for Brinkman when he comes.'

'That will be a thoroughly typical scene. And are you

taking poor Mr Pulteney to the post of honour and of danger?'

'If Mr Pulteney does not object. He knows his way about the garage.'

'I shall be delighted to go where glory waits. If I fall, I hope that you will put up a plain but tasteful monument over me, indicating that I died doing somebody else's duty.'

'And what about your two men?' asked Bredon.

'One of them will be told off to watch Simmonds. As I told you, I can't afford to leave Simmonds out of account. The other will wait out at the back, in a place I have selected; if (or rather when) Brinkman comes out at the back-door to make his way to the garage, my man will follow him at a distance, and will take his post at the garage door, in case there's any rough work there. That, I think, accounts for the whole party.'

'How long does our vigil last?' asked Eames.

'Not, I imagine, beyond nine o'clock. That is the hour at which the garage shuts; and, although there is a bell by which the proprietor can be fetched out if necessary, I hardly think that Brinkman would take the risk. The dusk is closing early this evening, with all these clouds about; and if, as I strongly suspect, there is a thunder-storm, it will be a capital night for his purpose. It's a nuisance for us, because I haven't dared to leave any of my watching-parties out of doors, for fear of a deluge.'

If tea had been an embarrassing meal, supper was a positive nightmare. But when the barmaid, carefully coached by Angela, asked for leave to go out to the pictures, a perfect piece of acting began. Angela's suggestion to her husband was beautifully done, so was his languid reply; Mr Pulteney excelled himself in the eagerness with which he offered to be her cavalier; Leyland's show of reluctance over the programme, and Eames' humorous resignation to his fate, completed the picture. Brinkman, after one nerve-racking pause, said he thought on the whole he would rather be excused. He found the cinema tiring to the eyes. 'Good,' said Bredon; 'then you and I will keep the home-fires burning. It's true I shall be sitting upstairs, because I've got my patience all laid out up there, and I haven't the heart to desert it. But if you're frightened of thunder, Mr Brinkman, you can always come up and have a crack with me.'

The alleged cinema party left at five minutes to eight. By that time Bredon was already immersed in his mysteries upstairs; and it was Brinkman, smilingly apologetic, who saw them off at the front-door. 'Don't sit up for us if we're late, Mr Brinkman,' said Angela, with the woman's instinct of overdoing an acted part; 'we'll throw brickbats in at my husband's window.' The inn door, with its ridiculous panes of blue and yellow, shut behind them, and they heard the unsuspecting footsteps of their victim climbing the stairs. As they passed down the street, a few drops of rain were falling, uneasy presages of the storm. Angela quickened her pace; she had not carried realism to the extent of arming herself with an umbrella. It was, in truth, but a short distance she and Eames had to travel; they were only just out of sight round a bend of the street when they doubled back upon the lane by which they were to return to the inn. At the entrance of it they met Emmeline, with the 'Boots' in attendance; it was difficult not to believe that, upon arrival at the cinema, he would be replaced by a more favoured escort. Leyland and Pulteney just stood long enough at the turning to make sure that all had gone well, and then continued their journey to the garage.

Here all was clearly in readiness; the proprietor was waiting for them at the door to receive his orders.

'Look here,' said Leyland, 'this gentleman and I are going to watch for a bit in here. Where's the telephone? Ah, that's all right; very well, we'll get behind this lorry. If anybody comes into the garage and wants you, he can ring that bell, can't he? And if anybody rings up on the telephone, we'll take the message; and if it's for you, not for us, we'll let you know. Meanwhile I suppose you and your mate can keep in the background?'

'That's all right, Sir, there won't be any difficulty about that. About how long might you be requiring the use of the garage for, Sir?'

'Till nine o'clock – that's your closing-time, isn't it? Any objections?'

'There ain't no difficulty, Sir, except that I've got to take my car out; I've got to meet a gentleman who's coming down on the 8.40 train. But if I take it straight out, and don't waste any time over it, that'll be all right, won't it? She's all ready for starting.'

'Very well. Twenty minutes to nine – or I suppose you'll want it about twenty-five to. Well, you may see us when you come back, or you may not. There's nothing else, then.'

As the proprietor withdrew behind the door which led into the workshop at the back, Leyland and Pulteney took up their stand behind a hay-waggon which afforded them generous concealment. Even as they did so, a sudden wink of lightning illuminated the outline of the garage and the road outside; it was followed by a distant roar of thunder. The wind had got up by now, and was moaning uneasily amongst the rafters of the building, which was no better than an open barn.

'Our performance could hardly have been better staged,' murmured the old gentleman. 'I only regret the absence of a revolver. Not that I should have any idea how to use a lethal weapon, but it would give me more sense of derring-do. It is singularly unfortunate that, even if I narrate the events of this evening to my pupils next term, they will not believe me. They suspect any information which comes from such a source. To you, I suppose, this is an everyday affair?'

'Don't you believe it, Mr Pulteney. Most of a detective's life is spent sitting in an office filling up forms, like any bank-clerk. I've got a revolver with me myself, but I'm not expecting any shooting. Brinkman doesn't strike me as being that kind of customer.'

'Is it intended that I should precipitate myself upon the miscreant and overpower him, or where exactly do my services come in?'

Leyland was rather at a loss to answer. The truth was, he did not quite trust Mr Pulteney, and he thought it best for that reason to keep him by his side. 'Well,' he said, 'two heads are better than one if it comes to a sudden alteration of plans. But there isn't going to be any difficulty about catching our friend. If he comes out by the back, he'll have my man shadowing him. If he should come out by the front, he will have Mr Eames shadowing him. So he will be caught between two fires.'

'But it might be difficult for Mr Eames to catch him if he were already in the motor-car and driving it.'

'Don't you worry about that, Mr Pulteney. I've fixed that car so that nobody's going to get her to move unless I want him to. It's the devil of a night, this. I hope Brinkman won't funk it.'

They seemed, indeed, to be in the very centre of a thunder-storm, though it was nowhere quite close at hand. Every few seconds, from some unexpected quarter, the whole sky seemed to wink twice in rapid succession, and with the wink the roofs of Chilthorpe would suddenly stand out silhouetted, and a pale glare fell on the white road outside. Storms of rain lashed upon the roof above them, and for a few minutes every gutter spouted and every seam in the tiles let in a pattering flood; then, without a word of warning, the rain would die down once more. Occasionally the lightning would manifest itself closer, great jagged streaks across the sky that looked as if they were burying themselves in the hill-summits above the town. When the elements were at rest for a moment, there was an uncanny stillness on every side; not a dog barked, not a footstep clattered down the deserted street.

Attuned as their nerves were to the roar of thunder, they both started as if in panic when the telephone-bell rang. Leyland was at the instrument in a moment, and heard Angela's cool voice asking for him at the other end.

'Is that you, Mr Leyland? Brinkman has just left the hotel by the front-door ... Yes, the *front*-door. I didn't see him myself, of course, but my husband said he came out quite coolly, just looking up at our window as if to see whether he was watched. Then I came straight to the telephone. I just looked in at the bar passage, and found that Mr Eames was not there, so I suppose he has followed. Shall I give any message to the man at the back? Oh, all right. ... Yes, he was carrying a dispatch-box, which looks as if he would round up with you before long. ... All right, we'll expect you when we see you.'

'That sounds all right,' said Leyland to his companion.

'We'd best take cover. Though why on earth the man came out by the front-door – Gad, he must be a cool customer! To walk out with his bag from the front-door, and wander in here asking for his car! Keep well behind the lorry, Mr Pulteney. ... Hullo, what's that?'

The door of the workshop opened, and the proprietor appeared, drawing on a pair of motoring-gloves. 'Sorry, Sir, it's twenty-five to; got to go and pick up my gent. Bad night for a drive, with the rain on your wind-screen, and this lightning blinding you every other second.'

'Hurry up, man, get clear,' said Leyland impatiently. 'He'll be here in a moment. As you come back, you might stop at the "Load of Mischief", because we may want a car.'

There was a drumming and a grinding, and the taxi bounded out on to the roadway. Leyland and Pulteney drew back behind the lorry, and waited for the sound of a footfall. They heard the hoot of the taxi as it passed the turning at the bridge; they heard the scrape as it changed gears a little later on the hill-road; then the noise died down, and there was silence. Two flashes of lightning, with the thunder following quick on them; then silence again. Five minutes passed, ten minutes, and still they sat on in the half-darkness. Leyland's mind was in a whirl of agitation. Granted that Brinkman had taken some circuitous route, to avoid observation, was it likely that he should take so long as this? He had had time to carry his luggage all round the township by now. ... Suddenly, from up the street, came a sound of running footsteps. Leyland gripped his revolver and waited with drawn breath.

CHAPTER 20

How Bredon Spent the Evening

BREDON had undoubtedly secured the best occupation for the evening. For two whole days he had missed the feeling of cards between his hands, and now he returned with a great hunger to his favourite pastime. True, the circumstances were not ideal. It was thoughtless of Leyland to have insisted on his sitting so close to the window; there was, fortunately, a window-seat, but not generous enough in its proportions to secure a convenient lay-out of the cards. The rows, instead of lying flat, had to climb over downs and gullies in the faded chintz; the result was an occasional avalanche, and a corresponding loss of temper. In an ideal world, Bredon reflected, you would have a large building like a racquet-court to play patience in, and you would wheel yourself up and down between the rows in an invalid's chair.

There was a soft rustle at the door, and Angela came in. 'Oo, I've been feeling so nice and stealthy,' she said. 'Mr Eames and I crept back down the lane just like burglars. It was better than a cinema, I can tell you. We dodged round the privet-hedge, and came in through the back of Mrs Davis's kitchen. And I thought the back stairs would never stop creaking. Did you hear me coming up?'

'I can't say I did. But, you see, I was otherwise engaged. To a man like Brinkman, on the alert for every noise, your progress probably sounded like a charge of cavalry. You're sure you shut the door properly? I need hardly say that a sudden draught would be a disaster to all my best hopes. A little knitting is indicated for you, Angela, to steady the mind.'

'Don't you talk too much. If Brinky came out and saw your lips moving, it might worry him. Remember, you're supposed to be alone in the room. Though indeed he probably regards you as potty by now in any case, so it wouldn't surprise him to see you talking to yourself.

Words cannot depict the shame I have felt this evening at having such a lazy husband. Talk of Nero fiddling while Rome was burning!'

'Say, rather, Drake insisting on finishing his game of bowls. Or was it William Tell? I forget. Anyhow, this is the fine old British spirit. What's the word? Not un-daunted – imperturbable, that's what I mean. The myrmi-dons of Scotland Yard bustle to and fro outside; the great detective sits calmly within, with all the strings in his hands. My nets begin to close tighter round them, Watson. Dash it all, I believe Pulteney's let me down. Where's his other two of spades?'

'I don't want to be unpleasant, but you will perhaps allow me to remind you that you are supposed to be on the look-out. If Brinky comes out in front, you are to report to me. And how are you to see him, if you will go scavenging about under the window-seat like that?'

'Well, you'll jolly well have to find my two of spades, then, while I keep an eye on the street. Fair division of labour. Watchman, what of the night? There's going to be a jolly fine thunder-storm. Did you see that flash? I deduce that there will shortly be a slight roll of thunder. There, what did I tell you?'

'It's not so much the innate laziness of the man,' murmured Angela, as if to herself, 'it's his self-sufficiency. Here's your beastly two of spades; don't lose it again. You ought to have the cards tied round your neck with a piece of string. I say, aren't you excited? Do you think Brinky will show fight when they nab him in the garage?'

'Don't fluster me. I wish to be secluded from the world. Here before me lies a very pretty problem, represented by two hundred and eight pieces of pasteboard. Behind that, in the dim background of my half-awake conscious-ness, lies a very pretty problem in detection. It is my boast that I can do both at once. But how am I to do either, if women will chatter at me?'

'Passengers are requested not to speak to the man at the wheel. All right, Aunty, go on with your silly game. I'm going to knit. It doesn't feel quite womanly to knit, some-how, with a thing like you in the room.'

There was silence for a while, as Bredon sat over his cards, with an occasional glance at the street below him. There is said to be a man who has invented a Chinese typewriter; and since (they tell us) every word in the Chinese language has its own symbol – the fault of Confucius, for not thinking of letters – the machine is said to be the size and shape of a vast organ, and the typist runs to and fro, pulling out a stop here, pressing down a pedal there, in a whirl of activity. Not otherwise did Bredon appear when he saw the possibilities of a particular gambit in his patience; then he would sit for a while lost in thought, puzzling out combinations for the future. Below him, the street lay in an unearthly half-darkness. Lamps should not have been needed by this time on a June evening, but the thick mantle of clouds had taken away all that was left of the sun's departing influence, and it was a twilit world that lay below. He could see a broad splash of light from the front-door, and, farther along, the mellower radiance diffused by the bar windows, with their drawn red blinds. From time to time a sudden flare of lightning illuminated the whole prospect, and shamed these human lights into insignificance.

'Angela,' said Bredon suddenly, without turning round, 'I don't know if it interests you at all, but a stealthy figure has crept out into the moonlight. At least, there isn't any moonlight, but still – Those irritatingly twirled moustaches, those supercilious pince-nez – can it be? It is – our old friend Brinkman. He carries a dispatch-box, but no other luggage. He is passing down the street in the direction of the turning; perhaps making for the garage – who shall say? He is looking round at this window; ha! 'tis well, I am observed. Anyhow, it's up to you to go to the telephone this time.'

Angela's self-possession was more of a pose. She sprang up in a hurry, dropping her knitting as she rose, and threw the door open silently but swiftly; then, as silently, as swiftly, it shut again behind her. But not before irretrievable damage had been done. The evening was full of those sudden gusts and air-currents which a thunderstorm brings with it. One of these, synchronizing with the sudden opening of the door, neatly lifted up three of the cards from the window-seat, and swept them out into the open air.

Bredon was intensely annoyed, and somewhat puzzled as to his duty. On the one hand, it was impossible to go on with the game when three cards, whose values he could not remember, were missing from a row. On the other hand, Leyland's instructions had been explicit; he was to sit at the window without stirring. Then common sense came to his aid. After all, Brinkman was no longer in sight; even if he were still watching from the corner, he would never suspect that a movement in the room upstairs portended discovery. With a great effort Bredon heaved himself up from the chair into which he had sunk, opened the door delicately for fear of fresh draughts, and in half a minute's time was searching before the front of the inn for his truant pasteboard.

The king of spades, good. And here was the three of diamonds. But there was one card; he was certain of it. A friendly flash of lightning gave him a sudden snap-shot of the road; Brinkman was out of sight; another figure, Eames presumably, was already making for the turning. But there was no card in the street; no deceptive fragments of paper, even, to catch the eye. He looked round, baffled. Then his eye caught the sight of an open groundfloor window, that of the best room. Could the fluttering runaway have dived indoors again? He put his head in through the window; there it lay, close to the occasional table with the photograph album on it. He was back through the front door in an instant, and making his way upstairs again with his prize.

'Great Scott!' he said, aloud, as he regained his room, 'could that possibly be it? That would mean, of course ... hang it all, what would that mean? Ah! That's more like it.' The patience lay all round him, forgotten for the moment; his eyes sparkled, his hands gripped the arms of his chair.

When Angela came back from the telephone, she was astonished at the change that had come over her husband. He was standing on the fender with his back to the empty grate, swinging himself to and fro while he carolled snatches from an out-of-date musical repertoire:

All the girls began to cry, Hi, hi, hi, Mister Mackay, Take us
with you when you fly back to the Isle of Skye,

were the actual words that greeted her entrance. 'Miles,
dear,' she expostulated, 'whatever's the matter? Have you
got it out?'

'What, the patience? No, I don't think the patience is
coming out just yet. But I've got a very strong suspicion
that our little detective mystery is coming out. As you are
up, I wonder if it would be troubling you too much to ask
you to step down to Mrs Davis and ask her if she ever
cut any sandwiches for Mr Brinkman?'

'My poor, poor dear!' said Angela; but she went. She
knew the signs of a victory in her husband's erratic deport-
ment. He was still crooning softly to himself when she
came back with her message.

'Mrs Davis says that she doesn't remember ever to have
cut any sangwiches, not for Mr Brinkman she didn't.
Mr Pulteney, now, he often takes a nice sangwich with him
when he goes out fishing. Not that she always makes them
herself, because the girl cuts as nice a sangwich as you'd
wish to see. But Mr Brinkman he didn't order any sangwiches, not all this week he hasn't. That's all the message.
At least, I came away at that point.'

'Good! The case progresses. Let me call your attention
to this singular absence of sangwich-cutting on the part of
Mrs Davis. Angela, I'm right on the track of the beastly
thing, and you mustn't disturb me.'

'Have you really worked it all out?'

'No, not quite all; but I'm in the sort of stage where
the great detective says, Good God, what a blind bat I
have been! As a matter of fact, I don't think I've been a
blind bat at all; on the contrary, I think it's dashed clever
of me to have got hold of the thing now. It's more than
you have.'

'Miles, you're not to be odious. Tell me all about it, and
I'll see what I think of you.'

'Who was it laughed at me for staying at home and
playing patience while other people did the work? No,
you shan't hear about it; besides, I haven't fitted it all
together yet.'

'Well, anyhow, you might tell me whether you've won the forty quid or lost it.'

'Not a word shall you get out of me at present.'

'Then I'll make Mr Leyland arrest you and torture you with thumbscrews. By the way, I wonder what Mr Leyland's doing? Brinky must have got to the garage by now, and I should have thought he would have brought him straight back here.'

'The garage? Oh, yes. At least, wait a minute ... Of course, now I come to think of it, there's no real reason to suppose that Brinkman meant to take the car out at all.'

CHAPTER 21

How Eames Spent the Evening

EAMES stood behind the window of the passage into the bar-parlour, making sure that there was no light behind him to show up his silhouette. Yes, there was no doubt, it was Brinkman who had stepped out into the twilight of the street; Brinkman with a dispatch-box in his hand; Brinkman on the run. He waited until the street-corner hid the fugitive from view, then crammed on his soft hat and followed. He was not an expert at this sort of game, but fortunately there was not much to be done. Brinkman would obviously make for the garage, and when he had passed through the open doors of it, it would be easy for him, Eames, to slink up behind and post himself outside the gateway to prevent a sudden rush. Hang it all, though, why hadn't the man gone out by the back lane?

And then he saw that he had counted on his luck too soon. Brinkman had reached the turning, and had not made for the garage after all. He had turned his back on it, and was starting out on the Pullford Road, the road towards the gorge and the Long Pool. This was outside all their calculations; what on earth could the man be up to? Not only was he deserting his car, he was deserting the garage, and with it all the available petrol-power of Chilthorpe. He could not be walking to Pullford, a distance of twenty miles, more or less. He could hardly even be walking to Lowgill Junction, eight miles off, though that would, of course, bring him on to the main line. Chilthorpe station would be hopeless at this time of night; no strand remained to connect it with civilization. No, if Brinkman took this road, he must be taking it only to return along it.

And yet, was it safe to reckon on that? Was it safe to make straight for the garage, and warn Leyland of what was happening? If he did that, he must let Brinkman out of his sight; and his orders were not to let Brinkman out of his sight. Eames was in the habit of obeying orders, and he obeyed. It would need cautious going, for, if Brinkman turned in his tracks, it was not unlikely that he would walk straight into the arms of his pursuer. Very cautiously, then, flattening himself in doorways or hiding behind clumps of broom and furze on the road-side, Eames stalked his man at a distance of some thirty yards. It was difficult work in the half-darkness, but those sudden, revealing flashes of lightning made it unsafe to go nearer. They had left the last of the houses, and were now reaching the forked roads a little way up the hill. If Brinkman took the lower road, it must be Lowgill Junction he was making for; that would make easy work for his pursuers, who could ride him down in a fast motor. Surely it could not be that; surely he could not be turning his back on the motor and the thousand pounds!

No, he was not making for Lowgill. He took the hill-turning instead; that led either to the railway-station or across the moors to Pullford. In either case every step was taking the hunted man further away from help. 'If he goes as far as the first milestone,' Eames said to himself, 'I'll defy my orders and cut back to the garage, so that they can get the car out and follow him. Confound it all, what's the man doing now?'

Brinkman had left the high road, and was making his way deliberately down the field path that led to the gorge. This was worse than ever; the path was steep, and Eames, although he carried an electric torch which Bredon had lent him, did not dare to use it for fear of betraying himself. He could not guess the significance of this last move. There was no road Brinkman could be making for, unless he returned to this same road at the other end of the gorge, a few hundred yards higher up. Was it safe to wait at the beginning of the path? Was it safe to follow along the road, flanking his movements from above? Once more Eames had to fall back upon his orders. There was only one way of keeping his man in sight, and that was to stick to his heels. It would mean, probably, some nasty stumbles in the half-darkness, but it was too late to consider that. At least, the fir-trees and the bracken made it easier to follow unseen. And the fir-trees kept off a little of the rain, which was now driving fiercely upon his overcoat, and clogging the knees of his trousers with damp. Never mind, he had his orders.

Any kind of scenery achieves dignity in a thunderstorm; but rocky scenery in particular is ennobled by the combination. Under those quivering flashes, the two sides of the valley with the river running in between looked like the wings of a gigantic butterfly, shaking off the pitiless dew that was falling on them. The opening of the gorge itself, with the slant of the shadows as the lightning-glare failed to reach its depths, was like an illustration to the Inferno. The rain on the hill-side turned to diamond drops as it reflected the flashes; 'the fire ran along the ground,' thought Eames to himself. It was a sight to make a man forget his present occupations, if those occupations had been less pressing and less sinister.

Brinkman himself either did not carry a torch or did not use it. His pace was leisurely on the whole, though he seemed to quicken his step a little when the church clock struck half past eight. By that time he was already at the opening of the gorge. This took him out of sight, and Eames, secure in the cover which the dark tufts of fern afforded, ran forward over the spongy grass to creep up nearer to him. The gorge itself, ominous at all times, was particularly formidable under such skies as these. The half-light enabled you to see the path, but (to a man unaccustomed to his surroundings) suggested the permanent possibility of losing your foothold; and when the lightning came, it revealed the angry torrent beneath with unpleasant vividness. Fortunately the noise of the elements deadened the sound of your feet on the hard rock. Eames hesitated for one moment, and then followed along the narrow path that led up the gorge.

He could just see the dim figure that went before him as it reached the wider foothold at the middle of the gorge, where Brinkman and Bredon had interrupted their conversation to comment on the shape of the rocks. Then it halted, and Eames halted, too; he was now less than twenty yards behind, and he was at the last turn in the rock which could promise him any shelter from observation. He did well to halt, for while he stood there a huge tree of lightning seemed to flash out from the opposite side of the valley, and, for an interval which you could count in seconds, the whole landscape lay open to view as if in hard daylight.

Eames' eyes were riveted upon a single spot; he had thoughts for nothing but the sudden and inexplicable behaviour of Brinkman. In that flash, he saw the little man leaping up in the air, his right hand outstretched at full arm's length, as if to reach the top, or something behind the top, of that very ledge which, this morning, he had compared to the rack in a railway-carriage. Indeed, Brinkman himself looked not unlike some juvenile traveller who just cannot reach the parcel he wants to bring down, and must needs jump for it. What was the object of Brinkman's manoeuvre did not appear, nor even whether he was trying to take something down from the ledge or to put something on to it. But the grotesque attitude, momentarily revealed in that single spot-light of the thunder-storm, was perfectly unmistakable.

The prolonged glare left Eames momentarily blinded, like one who has just passed a car with very powerful headlights. When he saw clearly again, the dark figure under the ledge was gone. Could Brinkman have taken alarm? He had looked backwards after his absurd leap, like a man who felt he was pursued. In any case, Eames must press forward now, or he would lose his quarry altogether. ... By the time he had reached the ledge, a new flash came, and showed him, at the very end of the gorge, Brinkman running as if for his life. There was no more sense in concealment; he must mend his own pace, too; and that was impossible, on this narrow shelf of rock, unless he lit his torch. Lighting it, he took one look at the ledge towards which Brinkman had been jumping, and, from his superior height, saw without difficulty an envelope which looked as if it must be the explanation of Brinkman's gesture. He reached it with little trouble, put it in his pocket, and ran. As he ran he heard the hum of a motor's engine on the road above him.

The scramble up the bank at the further end of the gorge was less formidable than he had feared, for he kept his torch alight, and made a pace very creditable to his years. But even as he breasted the level of the roadway, he saw a car climbing the hill, doubtless carrying Brinkman with it. He cried to the driver to stop, but a volley of thunder drowned his utterance. He turned impotently, and began running down the hill; in ten minutes or so, at this pace, he should be at the garage. But as he ran, he took the envelope out of his pocket, and scanned its superscription by the light of his torch. It read: 'To his Lordship the Bishop of Pullford. Private and Confidential.' He thrust it away, wondering; but a short-winded man running has no taste for puzzles. Would it be any use turning in to the 'Load of Mischief', and letting somebody else carry his message the rest of the way? Hardly; and a double set of explanations would be a waste of precious time.

He reached the garage panting too heavily for speech, and, in answer to a challenge in Leyland's voice, turned his own torch on himself for identification. Then, leaning wearily against the front of the lorry, he blurted out his explanations. 'He's gone – motor-car – towards Pullford – couldn't stop him – better follow him up – didn't look a fast car – lost him at the gorge – take me with you, and I'll explain.'

'Yes, but curse it all, has he made for Pullford or for Lowgill? There's a side road. We must try Lowgill; we can telegraph from there, anyhow, and have him stopped. Hullo, who next?'

Angela had rushed in, hatless, to announce Bredon's cryptic observation about the car. She knew his mysterious moods, and felt that it was best to make straight for Leyland, especially as her car was the only fast one in the township. 'Right you are,' she said, when the situation had been outlined to her; 'I'll drive you both into Lowgill; jump up.'

'Mr Pulteney,' said Leyland, 'do you mind going to the stables at the back of the inn, to find my man who's waiting there? Tell him what's happened, say he's to get on to the telephone, break into the Post Office if necessary, and warn Pullford and Lowgill. He may just have time to head the man off. Oh, by the way, he won't know who you are; may take you for Brinkman. Say *Here we are again* loudly, do you mind, when you're outside the stable.'

'It will be a novel experience,' said Mr Pulteney.

CHAPTER 22

At a Standstill

IT was nearly eleven o'clock before Angela returned, and, since she resolutely refused to disclose anything about her movements unless Bredon divulged his theory, there were no explanations at all that night. 'It's not that I'm inquisitive,' she explained, 'but I do want to break you of that bad habit of obstinacy.' 'Well, well,' said Bredon, 'if you choose to drag my name in the dust, not to mention my car, by these midnight expeditions, there's no more to be said.' And no more was said.

They found Leyland already at breakfast when they came down. He had been up, he said, since six, making inquiries in every conceivable direction. 'I must say,' he added, 'it wasn't Mrs Bredon's fault we didn't catch our man last night.'

'The woman was reckless, I suppose, as usual?' asked Bredon.

'Oh, no,' said Angela in self-defence, 'I only got her going a little.'

'It's eight miles to Lowgill by the sign-posts,' said Leyland, 'and a little more in real life. Mrs Bredon did it – and, remember, the gradients are far worse than those on the Pullford road – in just over twelve minutes. But we'd no luck. The up-train from Lowgill – it's the only one of the big expresses that stops there – had just gone before we arrived. And, of course, we couldn't tell whether Brinkman had gone on it or not. His car passed us on the road, only a few hundred yards from the station, and we hadn't time to stop.'

'What car was he in?'

'That's the devilish part of it – I'm sorry, Mrs Bredon.'

'That's the damnable part of it,' amended Angela serenely. 'It was the car from the garage; and it sailed out at twenty-five minutes to nine, under Mr Leyland's nose. Even the sleuth-like brain of Mr Pulteney didn't realize what was happening.'

153

'You see,' explained Leyland, 'it was a very well
arranged plant. Brinkman had rung up earlier in the
afternoon, asking the garage to meet the late train which
gets into Chilthorpe at 8.40. He gave the name of Merrick.
The garage naturally asked no questions as to where the
message came from; they're always meeting that late
train. And, of course, they assumed that there was somebody *arriving* by that train. Then, when the man had got
a little way out of the town, just above the gorge there, he
was stopped on the road by a passenger with a dispatch-
box in his hand, who was walking in the direction of
Chilthorpe, as if coming from the station. He waved at
the car, and asked if it was for Mr Merrick; then he explained that he was in a great hurry, because he wanted
to catch the express at Lowgill. It was a perfectly normal
thing to want to do, and there wasn't much time to do it
in; so the man went all out, and just caught the express in
time. He didn't know who we were when we passed
him, and it wasn't till he got back to Chilthorpe that he
realized what he'd done. Meanwhile, who's to say whether
Brinkman stopped at Lowgill, or really got into the express?'

'Or took the later train back to Pullford?' suggested
Bredon.

'No, we kept a good look-out to see that he didn't do
that. But the other uncertainty remained, and it was fatal
to my plans. I sent word to London to have the train
watched when it got in, giving a description of Brinkman;
but of course that's never any use. In half an hour or so I
shall get a telegram from London to say they've found
nothing.'

'You couldn't have the express stopped down the line?'

'I'd have liked to, of course. But it's a mail train, and
it's always full of rich people in first-class carriages. Give
me a local train on a Saturday night, and I'll have it
stopped and searched and all the passengers held up for
two hours, and not so much as a letter to the papers about
it. But if you stop one of these big expresses on the chance
of heading off a criminal, and nothing comes of it, there'll
be questions asked in the House of Commons. And I was
in a bad position, you see. I can't prove that Brinkman

was a murderer. Not at present, anyhow. If he'd run off in Mottram's car, I could have arrested him for car-stealing, but he hadn't. Why, he even paid Mrs Davis's bill.'

'Do you mean to say he asked for his bill yesterday afternoon, and we never heard of it?'

'No, he calculated it out exactly, left a tip of two shillings for the barmaid, and went off, leaving the money on his chest-of-drawers.'

'What about his suit-case?'

'It wasn't his, it was Mottram's. He carried off all his own things in the dispatch-box. Apart from the fact that he gave a false name to the garage people his exit was quite *en règle*. And it's dangerous to stop a train and arrest a man like that. Added to which, it was perfectly possible that he was lying doggo at Lowgill.'

It was at this point that Mr Pulteney sailed into the room. The old gentleman was rubbing his hands briskly in the enjoyment of retrospect; he had scarce any need of breakfast, you would have said, so richly was he chewing the cud of his experiences overnight. 'What a day I have spent!' he exclaimed. 'I have examined a motor-car, and even opened part of its mechanism, without asking the owner's leave. I have been suspected of murder. I have sat up in an extremely draughty garage, waiting to pounce upon a criminal. And, to crown it all, I have approached a total stranger with the words *Here we are again*. Really, life has nothing more to offer me. But where is Mr Eames?'

'We took him to Lowgill with us,' explained Angela, 'and when he got there he insisted on taking the late train back to Pullford. He said he had something to talk over with the Bishop. He has left some pyjamas and a toothbrush here as hostages, and says he will look in on us in the course of the day to reclaim them. So you'll see him again.'

'A remarkable man. A shrewd judge of character. He recognized me at once as a man of reflection. God bless my soul! Do I understand that Mrs Davis has provided us with sausages?'

'It's wonderful, isn't it?' said Angela. 'She must have felt that the occasion had to be marked out somehow. And she was so pleased at having her bill paid. I don't think

Brinky can have been such an unpleasant man after all.'

'Believe me,' said Leyland earnestly, 'there is no greater mistake than to suppose your criminal is a man lost to all human feelings. It is perfectly possible for Brinkman to have murdered his master, and have been prepared to run off with a car and a thousand pounds which didn't belong to him, and yet to have shrunk from the prospect of leaving an honest woman like Mrs Davis the poorer for his visit. We are men, you see, and we are not made all in one piece.'

'But how odd of him to pop off into the gorge like that! I mean, it's a very jolly place, they tell me; and we know Brink admired the scenery of it, because he told my husband so. But isn't it rather odd of him to have wanted to take a long, last, lingering look at it before he bolted for South America?'

'It is perfectly possible that it may have had a fascination for him,' assented Leyland. 'But I think his conduct was more reasonable than you suppose. After all, by coming up at the further end of the gorge he managed to make it look quite natural when the motor found him walking in the direction of Chilthorpe. And, more than that, I have little doubt that he knew he was followed. Eames is a most capable fellow, but he must, I think, have followed his man a little carelessly, and so given himself away. Brinkman probably thought that it was Bredon who was following him.'

'Because he did it so badly, you mean?' suggested Angela. 'Miles, you shouldn't throw bread at breakfast; it's rude.'

'I didn't mean that. I meant that he had reason to believe Mr Eames was at the cinema, whereas he knew Bredon was in the house, and saw him sitting in a window that looks down over the street. Almost inevitably he must have supposed that it was the watcher in the front of the house who had followed in his tracks.'

'It's worse than that,' said Bredon. 'I'm afraid, you see, when my wife went out of the room, she opened the door in that careless way she has, and three of my cards fell into the street below. Well, I thought Brinkman had disappeared; there was no sign of him. So I went downstairs

156

and retrieved the cards, thinking it couldn't do any harm. But I've been wondering since whether Brinkman wasn't still watching, and whether my disappearance from the window didn't give him the first hint that he was being followed. I'm awfully sorry.'

'Well, I don't expect it made any difference. He was a cool hand, you see. I suppose he thought your sitting in the window must be a trap, and that the house was really watched at the back. He wasn't far wrong there, of course.'

'Indeed he was not,' assented Mr Pulteney. 'You seem to me to have posted a singularly lynx-eyed gentleman in the stables.'

'And so, you see, he thought he'd brazen it out. He reckoned on being followed, but that didn't matter to him as long as the man behind was a good distance off, and as long as he himself made sure of picking up his car at the right moment. The whole thing was monstrously mismanaged on my part. But, you see, I made absolutely certain that he was going for Mottram's car, in which he'd obviously made all the necessary preparations. Even now I can't understand how he consented so calmly to leave the car behind him. Unless, of course, he spotted that we were watching the garage, and knew that it would be unsafe. But he must be crippled for money without his thousand.'

'My husband,' said Angela mischievously, 'seemed to know beforehand that he wouldn't go off in Mottram's car.'

'Yes, by the way,' asked Leyland, 'how was that?'

'I'm sorry, it ought to have occurred to me earlier. It never dawned on me till the moment when I mentioned it, and of course then it was too late. But it was merely the result of a reasoning process which had been going on in my own mind. I had been trying to work things out, and it seemed to me that I had arrived at last at an explanation which would cover all the facts. And that explanation, though it didn't exclude the possibility that Brinkman intended to skip with the thousand and the car, didn't make it absolutely necessary that he should mean to.'

'I suppose you're still hankering after suicide?'

'I didn't say so.'

'But, hang it all, though there's little enough that's clear, it's surely clear by now that Brinkman was a wrong 'un. And if he was a wrong 'un, what can his motive have been throughout unless he was Mottram's murderer? I don't associate innocence with a sudden flitting at night-fall, and a bogus name given in when you order the car to take you to the station.'

'Still, it's not enough to have a general impression that a man is a wrong 'un, and hang him on the strength of it. You must discover a motive for which he would have done the murder, and a method by which he could have done it. Are you prepared to produce those?'

'Why, yes,' said Leyland. 'I don't profess to have all the details of the case at my fingers' ends; but I'm prepared to give what seems to me a rational explanation of all the circumstances. And it's an explanation which contends that Mottram met his death by murder.'

CHAPTER 23

Leyland's Account of it all

'OF course, as to the motive,' went on Leyland, 'I am not absolutely sure that I can point to a single one. But a combination of motives is sufficient, if they are comparatively strong ones. On the whole, I am inclined to put the thousand pounds first. For a rich man, Mottram did not pay his secretary very well; and at times, I understand, he talked of parting with him. Brinkman knew that the sum was in Mottram's possession, for it was he himself who cashed the cheque at the bank. It was only a day or two before they came down here. On the other hand, I doubt if Brinkman knew where the money was; plainly Mottram didn't trust him very much, or he wouldn't have taken the trouble to sew up the money in the cushions of the car. When I first found the *cache*, I assumed that Brinkman knew of its existence, and that was one of the reasons why I felt so certain that he would make straight for the garage. Now, I'm more inclined to think he fancied he would find the money among Mottram's effects, which he must have hoped to examine in the interval before the arrival of the police.'

'Then you don't think the Euthanasia had anything to do with it after all?' asked Bredon.

'I wouldn't say that. There's no doubt that Brinkman was a rabid anti-clerical – Eames was talking to me about that; and I think it's quite likely he would have welcomed, in any case, an opportunity of getting Mottram out of the way provided that the death looked like suicide. The appearance of suicide would have the advantage, as we have all seen, that the Indescribable wouldn't pay up. But he wanted, in any case, to give the murder the appearance of suicide, in order to save his own skin.'

'Then you think both motives were present to his mind?'

'Probably. I suppose there is little doubt that he knew of the danger to Mottram's health, and the consequent danger, from his point of view, that the money would go to the Pullford diocese. But I don't think that motive would have been sufficient, if he hadn't reckoned on getting away with a thousand pounds which didn't belong to him.'

'Well, let's pass the motive,' said Bredon. 'I'm interested to hear your account of the method.'

'Our mistake from the first has been that of not accepting the facts. We have tried to fit the facts into our scheme, instead of letting the facts themselves guide us. From the first, we were faced with what seemed to be a hopeless contradiction. The locked door seemed to make it certain that Mottram was alone when he died. The fact that the gas was turned off seemed to make it clear that Mottram was *not* alone when he died. There was ground for suspecting either suicide or murder; the difficulty was to make the whole complex of facts fit into either view. We had made a mistake, I repeat, in not taking the facts for our guide. The door was locked, that is a fact. Therefore Mottram was alone from the time he went to bed until the time when the door was broken in. And at the time when the door was broken in the gas was found turned off. Somebody must have turned it off, and in order to do so he must have been in the room. There was only one person in the room, Mottram. Therefore it was Mottram who turned the gas off.'

'You mean in his last dying moments?'

'No, such a theory would be fantastic. Mottram clearly turned the gas off in the ordinary way. Therefore *it was not the gas in Mottram's room which poisoned Mottram.*'

'But hang it all, if it wasn't in his room –'

'When I say that, I mean it was not the gas which turned on and off in Mottram's room. For that gas was turned off. Therefore it must have been some independent supply of gas which poisoned him.'

'Such as –?'

'Doesn't the solution occur to you yet? The room, remember, is very low, and the window rather high up in the wall. What is to prevent a supply of gas being introduced from outside and from above?'

'Good Lord! You don't mean you think that Brinkman –'

'Brinkman had the room immediately above. Since his hurried departure, I have had opportunities of taking a better look round it. I was making some experiments there early this morning. In the first place, I find that it is possible for a man leaning out of the window in Brinkman's room to control, with a stick, the position of the window in Mottram's room – provided always that the window is swinging loose. He can ensure at will that Mottram's window stands almost shut, or almost fully open.'

'Yes, I think that's true.'

'I find, further, that Brinkman's room, like Mottram's, was supplied with a double apparatus; with a bracket on the wall, and with a movable standard lamp. But whereas the main tap in Mottram's room was near the door, and the tube which connected the gas with the standard lamp was meant to allow the lamp to be put on the writing-table, in Brinkman's room it was the other way. The main tap was near the window, and the tube which connected it with the standard lamp was meant to allow the lamp to be placed by the bedside. The main tap in Brinkman's room is barely a yard from the window. And the tube of the standard lamp is some four yards long.

'When Mottram went to bed, Brinkman went up to his room. He knew that Mottram had taken a sleeping-draught; that in half an hour or so he would be asleep, and unconscious of all that went on. So, leaving a prudent interval of time, Brinkman proceeded as follows. He took the tube off from the foot of the standard lamp; that is quite an easy matter. Then he took the tube to the window. With a walking-stick he slightly opened Mottram's window down below – it had been left ajar. And through the opening thus made he let down the tube till the farther end of it was in Mottram's room. Then, with the walking-stick, he shut the window again, except for a mere crack which was needed to let the tube through. Then he turned on the guide-tap which fed his standard lamp, and the gas began to flow through into Mottram's room. That coil of tube was a venomous serpent, which could poison Mottram in his sleep, behind locked doors, and be removed again without leaving any trace when its deadly work was done.

'Whether it was through carelessness on Brinkman's part, or whether it was owing to the wind, that the window swung right open and became fixed there, I don't know. In any case, it did not make much difference to his plans. He had now succeeded in bringing off the murder, and in a way which it would have been hard for anybody to suspect. But there was one more difficulty to be got over. In order to remove the suspicion of murder, and to make the suspicion of suicide inevitable, it was necessary to turn on the gas in Mottram's room. Now, there was no implement Brinkman could employ which would enable him to reach Mottram's gas tap. He depended, therefore, on bluff. He made sure that he would be summoned by the Boots when the locked door forbade entrance. He would force his way in with the Boots; he would make straight for the tap, and *pretend* to turn it off. Would anybody doubt that it was he who had turned it off? The room was full of gas-fumes, and even a man of more intelligence than the Boots would naturally leap to the conclusion that the gas *must* have been on, in order to account for the fumes.

'His plan, you see, was perfect in its preparations. It was an unexpected interference that prevented its coming off. When Brinkman was telling you the story, he pretended that it was he who saw Dr Ferrers outside, and suggested calling him in. Actually it was the Boots, according to the story he himself tells, who drew attention to the presence of Dr Ferrers and suggested his being called in. This point, which was of capital importance, was slurred over at the inquest because nobody saw the bearing of it. Brinkman did not much want Dr Ferrers to be there; yet the suggestion was too reasonable to be turned down. Brinkman stationed himself with his shoulder close to the lock, while Ferrers leant his weight against the door at the other end, nearest the hinges. Assuming that the lock would give, Brinkman could rush into the room first and go through the motions of turning off the gas without attracting suspicion.

'Actually, it was the hinges which gave. Dr Ferrers, realizing that the gas must be turned off in order to clear the air, ran straight to the tap over the débris of the broken door, before Brinkman could get at it. And Ferrers naturally exclaimed in surprise when he found the tap already turned off. The Boots heard his exclamation; Brinkman's plan had fallen through. There was nothing for it but to pretend that the tap was a loose one, and that Dr Ferrers had himself turned it off without noticing it. That was the story, Bredon, which he put up to you. We know that it was a lie.'

'I don't quite see,' said Bredon, 'how all this works in with the sandwiches and whisky. In the motor, I mean. What was the idea of them?'

'Well, Brinkman's original idea must clearly have been flight. That was, I take it, when he realized the difficulty which had been created for him by his failure to reach the gas first. It must have been before I arrived that he made these preparations – stored the motor with food and painted out the number-plate at the back. I've had him under pretty careful observation ever since I came here. But that was Tuesday afternoon, and I have no doubt that his preparations had been made by then.'

'And why didn't he skip?'

'I think he was worried by my arrival. You see, he tried to palm off the suicide story on me, and I didn't fall to it. If he skipped, he would confirm me in my conviction there had been a murder, and, although he himself might get off scot-free, it would mean that your Indescribable people would have to pay up to the Bishop of Pullford. He couldn't stand the idea of that. He preferred to hang about here, trying to convince you, because you were already half-convinced, that the case was one of suicide and that the Company were not liable.'

'In fact, he just waited for the funeral, and then made off?'

'No, he waited until he thought he wasn't watched. It's a rum business, shadowing a man; you don't want him to see exactly who is shadowing him, or where the man is who is shadowing him; but you do, very often, want him to know that he is shadowed, because that makes him lose his head and give himself away. Now, Brinkman didn't know what I suspected and didn't, I think, know about my two men at the "Swan". But I contrived to let him see that he was under observation, and that it wasn't safe for him to go far out of my sight. It's an old game, you give a man that impression, and then you suddenly let on that he is free – for the moment at any rate. He seizes his chance, and, with luck, you catch him. He really thought yesterday evening that you were the only person watching the front of the house. But he was clever enough, confound him, to see that there might be danger for him in the garage. So he rang up, ordering a car to meet the 8.40 at Chilthorpe Station, and then made his arrangements – uncommonly good ones – for boarding the car *en route*. And nobody's to blame, exactly, but I gravely fear that the murderer has got off scot-free.'

As if in confirmation of his words, the maid came in with a telegram. He opened it and crushed it in his hand. 'As I thought,' he said; 'they searched the train at the terminus and didn't find their man. They may watch the ports, but I doubt if they'll get him now. It's a rotten business.'

'I don't think you've explained everything,' said Bredon, 'I mean, about Brinkman's movements after the murder. Indeed, I know for a fact that you haven't explained everything; partly because you don't know everything. But I think your account of Brinkman's movements that night is extraordinarily ingenious, and I only wish it were true. I wish it were true, I mean, because it would have brought us up, for once in our lives, against a really clever criminal. But, you see, there's one thing which is fatal to all your theory. You haven't explained why the gas-tap showed the mark where Mottram turned it on, and didn't show the mark where Mottram turned it off.'

'Oh, yes, I admit that's puzzling. Still, one can imagine circumstances –'

'One can imagine circumstances, but one can't fit them on to the facts. If the gas had been quite close to Mottram's bed, and he had had a stick by his side, he might have turned off the tap with the stick; I've known slack men do that. But the gas wasn't near enough for that. Or, again, if Mottram had gone to bed in gloves, he might have turned off the tap with gloves on; but he didn't. The tap was stiff; it was stiff both when you turned it on and when you turned it off; and there must, in reason, have been some slight trace left if that gas was turned off by a man's naked fingers. Therefore it wasn't turned off by a man's naked fingers. Therefore it wasn't turned off by Mottram, or by anybody who had any business to turn it off. It was turned off by somebody who had a secret end to serve in doing so.'

'You mean a criminal end?'

'I didn't say that. I said a secret end. Your view doesn't explain that; and because it doesn't explain that, although I think you've told us an extraordinarily ingenious story, I don't think it's worth forty pounds. ... Hullo! What's this arriving?'

The taxi from the garage had drawn up outside the inn-door, and was depositing some passengers, who had obviously come by the early morning train from Pullford. They were not left in doubt for long; the coffee-room door was opened, and, with 'Don't get up, please,' written all over his apologetic features, the Bishop of Pullford walked in. Eames followed behind him.

'Good morning, Mr Bredon. I'm so sorry to disturb you and your friends at breakfast like this. But Mr Eames here has been telling me about your alarums and excursions last night; and I thought probably there would be some tired brains this morning. Also, I felt it was important to tell you all I know, because of Mr Brinkman's hurried departure.'

Bredon hastily effected the necessary introductions. 'You know something, then, after all?'

'Oh, you mustn't think I've been playing you false, Mr Bredon. The evidence I'm referring to only came to hand last night. But such as it is, it's decisive; it proves that poor Mottram met his death by suicide.'

CHAPTER 24

Mottram's Account of it all

'RAPID adjustment of the mental perspective,' said Mr Pulteney, 'is an invaluable exercise, especially at my age. But I confess there is a point at which the process becomes confusing. Are we now to understand that Mr Brinkman, so far from being a murderer, is simply an innocent man with a taste for motoring late at night? I have no doubt there is a satisfactory explanation of it all, but it looks to me as if there had been an absence of straightforwardness on somebody's part.'

'Possibly on that of Mr Eames,' said the Bishop. 'I have to confess, on his behalf, that he has been concealing something, and to take the blame for his conduct – if blame attaches to it – unreservedly upon myself. However, I do not think that any earlier disclosure could have helped forward the cause of justice; and I have lost no time in putting it all before you.'

'You mean that letter which was left about in the gorge,' suggested Bredon, 'addressed to the Bishop of Pullford? With a confession of suicide in it?'

'Goodness, Mr Bredon, you seem to know as much about it as I do myself! Well, that is the long and short of it. When Mr Eames was with you last night, Mr Leyland, he told you that he had followed Brinkman along the gorge, and that Brinkman had disappeared in a motor. He did not tell you that, half-way through the gorge, he saw Brinkman leaping up under a ledge in the rock, as if to put something on it or take something down from it. The something which he was putting up or taking down was, I make no doubt, the document which I now hold in my hand. Mr Eames found it after Brinkman had left, and seeing that it was addressed to me with an intimation that it was private and confidential, thought it best to carry it straight to me without informing you of its existence. I understood him to say that he did not mention its existence to you, Mr Bredon, either.'

'Nor did I,' put in Eames.

'How jolly of you, Mr Eames,' said Angela. 'You can't think what a lot of trouble we've been having with my husband; he thinks he knows all about the mystery, and he won't tell us; isn't it odious of him? And I'm so glad to think that you managed to keep him in the dark about something.'

'Not entirely,' protested Bredon. 'Cast your eye over that, Mr Eames.' And a document was handed, first to Eames, then to the rest of the company, which certainly seemed to make Eames' caution unnecessary. It was a plain scrap of paper, scrawled over in pencil with the handwriting of a man who is travelling at thirty-five miles an hour over bumpy roads in a badly-sprung car. All it said was: Make Eames show you what he found in the gorge. I thought it was you. – F. Brinkman.

'Ah!' said the Bishop. 'Brinkman, it seemed, had some doubt as to the fate of a document which got into the hands of the Catholic authorities. Poor fellow, he was always rather bitter about it. However, here we are, Mr Bredon, owning up like good boys. It was to put that very document into your hands that I came down this morning. But I think Mr Eames was quite right in holding that the document, with such a superscription, ought to be handed over to me direct, without any mention even of its existence to a third party.'

'I for one,' put in Leyland, 'applaud his action. I do not believe in all these posthumous revelations; I prefer to respect the confidence of the dead. But I understand that your Lordship is prepared to let us see the contents of the letter after all?'

'Certainly. I think poor Mottram's last directions were influenced simply by consideration for my own feelings in the matter. I have no hesitation, myself, in making it public. Shall I read it here and now?'

In deference to a chorus of assent, the Bishop took out the enclosure of the envelope and prepared to read. 'I ought to say by way of preface,' he explained, 'that I knew poor Mottram's handwriting well enough, and I feel fully convinced that this is a genuine autograph of his, not a forgery. You will see why I mention that later on.

This is how the letter runs:

'MY DEAR LORD BISHOP,

'Pursuant to our conversation of Thursday evening last, it will be within your Lordship's memory that upon that occasion I asserted the right of a man, in given circumstances, to take his own life, particularly when same was threatened by an incurable and painful disease. This I only mentioned casually, when illustrating the argument I was then trying to put forward, namely that the end justifies the means, even in a case where said means are bad, provided said ends are good. I note that your Lordship is of the contrary opinion, namely that said end does not justify said means. I am, however, confident that in a concrete case like the present your Lordship will be more open to conviction *re* this matter, as it is a case where I am acting to the best of my lights, which, your Lordship has often told me, is all that a man can do when in doubtful circumstances.

'I regret to have to inform your Lordship that, interviewing recently a specialist in London *re* my health, said specialist informed me that I was suffering from an incurable disease. I have not the skill to write the name of it; and as it is of an unusual nature, maybe it would not interest your Lordship to know it. The specialist was, however, of the decided opinion that I could not survive more than two years or thereabouts; and that in the interim the disease would give rise to considerable pain. It is therefore my intention, in pursuance of the line of argument which I have already done my best to explain to your Lordship, to take my own life, in circumstances which will be sufficiently public by the time this reaches you.

'I have not, as your Lordship knows, any firm religious convictions. I believe that there is a future life of some kind, and that we shall all be judged according to our opportunities and the use we made of same. I believe that God is merciful, and will make allowances for the difficulties we had in knowing what was the right thing to do and in doing it. But I have been through some hard times, and maybe not always acted for the best. Being desirous, therefore, of making my peace with God, I have taken the liberty of devising some of the property of which I die possessed to your Lordship personally, to be used for the benefit of the diocese of Pullford. Said property consisting of the benefits accruing from the Euthanasia policy taken out by me with the Indescribable Insurance Company. And so have directed my lawyers in a will made by me recently.

'I believe that your Lordship is a man of God, and anxious to do his best for his fellow-citizens in the town of Pullford. I believe that the money will serve a good end, although I do not agree

168

with what your Lordship teaches. I feel sure that your Lordship
will realize the desirability of keeping this letter private, and not
letting it be known that I took my own life. The Insurance
Company would probably refuse to pay the claim if I were
supposed to have died by my own hand, that being their rule
in such cases, except where the deceased was of unsound mind,
which is not the case, me being in full possession of all my facul-
ties. If, however, the preparations which I have made should
eventuate successfully, it will not be supposed by the Coroner's
jury that I took my own life, and the claim will be paid accordingly. Your Lordship will realize that this is only fair, since
(1) in taking my own life I am only anticipating the decree of
Nature by a few months, and (2) the object to which I have
devised the money is not the selfish enjoyment of a few persons,
but the spiritual benefit of a large number, mostly poor. I am
writing this, therefore, for your Lordship's own eye, and it has
no need to be made public. I am quite sure that God will forgive me what I am doing if it is at all wrong, for I am afraid
to suffer pain and am doing my best to bequeath my money in
such a way that same will be used for good purposes. With
every gratitude for the kindness I have always received at
Cathedral House, though not of the same religion, I remain,

'Your Lordship's obedient servant,

'J. MOTTRAM'

The Bishop's voice quavered a little at certain points
in this recital; it was difficult not to be affected by the
laborious efforts of a pen untrained in language to do
justice to the writer's friendly intentions. 'I'm very sorry
indeed for the poor fellow,' he said. 'The older we grow,
the more tender we must become towards the strange
vagaries of the human conscience. That's not the letter of
a man whose mind is unhinged. And yet what is one to
make of a conscience so strangely misformed? However, I
didn't come here to talk about all that. You'll see for
yourselves that, although the writer *recommends* my keeping
it dark, he places me under no obligation to do so – he
would have put me in an uncommonly awkward position
if he had. As it is, I've had no hesitation in reading it to
you, and shall have no hesitation in producing it, if necessary, before a court of law. It seems that our legacy, after
all, was only a castle in Spain.'

'The poor dear!' said Angela. 'And it's bad luck on
you, Mr Leyland. Did you realize, my Lord, that Mr

169

Leyland had just succeeded in persuading us all that Mr Brinkman had murdered Mr Mottram by letting in gas from the room above?'

'Well, thank God it was nothing as bad as that!' said the Bishop. 'At least this letter will help us to take a kindlier view of him.'

'It would,' said Mr Pulteney, 'be a very singular and, I had almost said, a diverting circumstance, if both things could have happened at once – if, while Mottram was busy poisoning himself with his own gas down below, Brinkman was at the same moment, in complete ignorance, feeding him with an extra supply of gas from above. It would be a somewhat knotty problem, in that case, to decide whether we were to call it suicide or murder. However,' he added with a little bow to the Bishop, 'we have a competent authority with us.'

'Oh, don't ask me, sir,' protested the Bishop, 'I should have to consult my Canon Penitentiary. He would tell me, I fancy, that the act of murder in this case *inflowed* into the act of suicide, but I am not sure that would help us much.'

'Perhaps,' suggested Eames, 'Mr Bredon could tell us what view the Indescribable would take of such a case.'

'They would be hard put to it,' said Bredon. 'Fortunately, there is no question of any such doubt here. For Leyland's suggestion of murder was only based on the impossibility of suicide, in view of the gas being turned off. Whereas Mr Pulteney's ingenious suggestion has all the difficulties in it which Leyland was trying to avoid.'

'I'm hanged if I can make head or tail of it,' said Leyland. 'It's like a nightmare, this case; every time you think you've found some solid ground to rest on, it sinks under your feet. I shall begin to believe in ghosts soon. And what are we to make of the message itself? Might I see the envelope, my Lord? ... Thank you. Well, it's clear that Brinkman wasn't putting the letter up on the ledge; he was taking it down. It's so weather-stained that it must clearly have been there the best part of a week. Now, why on earth was Brinkman so anxious to take the letter away with him? For the letter proved it was suicide, and that's precisely what he wanted to have proved.'

'Brinkman may not have known what was in the letter,' suggested Eames.

'He may have thought the thousand pounds were in it,' suggested Pulteney, 'waiting there as a surprise present for the Bishop. I am no acrobat myself, but I believe I could jump pretty high if you gave me that sum to aspire to.'

'I wonder if Brinkman did know?' said Leyland. 'Of course, if he did, he was an accessory before the fact to Mottram's suicide. And that might make him anxious for his own position – but it doesn't ring true, that idea.'

'Might I see the letter itself?' asked Bredon. 'It sounds impolite, I know; but I only want to look at the way in which it's written ... Thank you, my Lord. ... It's rather a suggestive fact, isn't it, that this letter was copied?'

'Copied?' asked the Bishop. 'How on earth can you tell that?'

'I am comparing it in my mind's eye with the letter we found lying about in Mottram's bedroom, half finished. Mottram wrote with difficulty, his thoughts didn't flow to his pen. Consequently, in that letter to the *Pullford Examiner*, you will find that only the last sentence at the bottom of the page has been blotted when the ink was wet. The rest of the page had had time to dry naturally, while Mottram was thinking of what to say next. But this letter of yours, my Lord, has been written straight off, and the blotting process becomes more and more marked the further you get down the page. I say, therefore, that Mottram had already composed the letter in rough, and when he sat down to this sheet of paper he was copying it straight down.'

'You're not suggesting that Brinkman dictated the letter?' asked Leyland. 'Of course, that would open up some interesting possibilities.'

'No, I wasn't thinking of that. I was only thinking it was rather a cold-blooded way for a suicide to write his last letter. But it's a small point.'

'And meanwhile,' said Leyland, 'I suppose you're waiting for me to fork out those forty pounds?'

'What,' said the Bishop, 'you have a personal interest in this, Mr Bredon? Well, in any case you have saved your company a larger sum than that. I'm afraid you will have to write and tell them that it was suicide, and the claim does not urge.'

'On the contrary, my Lord,' said Bredon, knocking out his pipe thoughtfully into the fireplace, 'I'm going to write to the Company and tell them that the claim has got to be paid, because Mottram met his death by accident.'

CHAPTER 25

Bredon's Account of it all

'GOD bless my soul!' cried the Bishop, 'you don't mean to say you're preparing to hush it up! Why, your moral theology must be as bad as poor Mottram's.'

'It isn't a question of theology,' replied Bredon, 'it's a question of fact. I am going to write to the Indescribable Company and tell them that Mottram died by accident, because that happens to be the truth.'

'Ah-h-!' said Angela.

'Indeed?' said Mr Eames.

'Not another mental perspective!' groaned Mr Pulteney.

'That's exactly what it is. I'm not a detective really; I can't sit down and think things out. I see everything just as other people do, I share all their bewilderment. But suddenly, when I'm thinking of something quite different, a game of patience, for example, I see the whole thing in a new mental perspective. It's like the optical illusion of the tumbling cubes – you know, the pattern of cubes which looks concave to the eye; and then, by a readjustment of your mental focus, you suddenly see them as convex instead. What produces that change? Why, you catch sight of one particular angle in a new light, and from that you get your new mental picture of the whole pattern. Just so, one can stumble upon a new mental perspective about a problem like this by suddenly seeing one single fact in a new light. And then the whole problem re-arranges itself.'

'I am indebted to you for your lucid exposition,' said Mr Pulteney, 'but even now the events of the past week are not quite clear to me.'

'Miles, don't be tiresome,' said Angela. 'Start right from the beginning and don't let's have any mystery-making.'

'All right. It would make a better story the other way, but still. Well, first you want to get some picture of Mottram. I can only do it by guess-work, but I should say this. He had an enormous amount of money, and no heir whom he cared for. He was a shrewd, rather grasping man, and he came to think that everybody else was after his money. It's not uncommon with rich people – what you might call the Chuzzlewit-complex. Am I right so far?'

'Absolutely right,' said the Bishop.

'Again, he was a man who loved a mystery for its own sake, surprises, almost practical jokes. And again, he was a vain man in some ways, caring intensely what other people thought of him, and very anxious to know what they thought of him. Also, he had a high respect for the Catholic Church, or at least for its representatives in Pull-ford.'

'All that's true,' said Eames.

'Well, I think he really did mean to leave some money to the Pullford diocese. No, don't interrupt; that's not as obvious as it sounds. He really did mean to endow the diocese, and he disclosed his intention to Brinkman. Brinkman, as we know, was a real anti-clerical, and he protested violently. Catholics were alike, he said, all the world over; the apparent honesty of a man like your Lordship was only a blind. In reality, Catholics, and especially Catholic priests, were always hunting for money and would do anything to get it – anything. At last Mottram determined that he must settle the point for himself. First of all, he went round to Cathedral House and defended the proposition that it was lawful to do evil in order that good might come. He wanted to see whether he would get any support for that view in the abstract; he got none. Then he decided, with Brinkman's collabo-ration, on a practical test. He would put your Lordship's honesty to the proof.

'He went up to London, saw his solicitors, and added a codicil to his will, leaving the benefits of the Euthanasia policy to the Bishop of Pullford. I am afraid it must be admitted that he did not, at the time, mean that codicil to become operative. It was part of his mystery. Then he went on to our people at the Euthanasia, and spun a cock-and-bull yarn about seeing a specialist, who had told him that he had only two more years to live. Actually he was in robust health; he only invented this story and told it to the Indescribable in order that, when it came to the point, it might be reasonable (though not necessary) to explain his death as suicide. Then he came back here and made preparations for his holiday. He was going to take his holiday at Chilthorpe – to be more accurate, he meant to start his holiday at Chilthorpe. He strongly urged your Lordship to come down and share part of it with him; it was essential to his plan.'

'And that,' suggested the Bishop, 'explains his intense eagerness that I should come down?'

'Precisely. He made certain, as best he could, that you would arrive here on the morning after him; that you would be told he had gone out to fish the Long Pool, and that you would be asked to follow him. This would ensure that you would be the first witness of his disappearance.'

'His what?'

'His disappearance. He meant to disappear. Not only for the sake of the test, I imagine; he wanted to disappear for the fun of the thing; to see what happened. He wanted to be a celebrity in the newspapers. He wanted to read his own biographies. That was why he wrote, or rather got Brinkman to write, a letter to the *Pullford Examiner*, calling him all sorts of names – the letter was signed, of course, with a pseudonym. You found that out, didn't you, Leyland?'

'Yes, confound it all, I heard only this morning that "Brutus" was really Brinkman. But I never saw the point.'

'Then he sat down and wrote an unfinished letter in answer to these charges. That letter, of course, was to be found after his disappearance, and would be published in thick type by the *Pullford Examiner*. That would set everybody talking about him, and his obituary notices would be lively reading. He wanted to read them himself. But in order to do that he must disappear.

'Chilthorpe gorge is a good place to disappear from. Leave your hat on the edge of it, and go and hide somewhere – you will be reported the next morning as a tragic accident. Mottram had made all arrangements for hiding. He was going to spend his holiday *incognito* somewhere; I think in Ireland, but it may have been on the Continent.

He was going to take Brinkman with him. He would disappear, of course, in his car. He had victualled it before he left Pullford. On his arrival at Chilthorpe his first act was to paint out its number-plate. He hid some notes in the cushions of the car – that, I think, was a mere instinct of secretiveness; there was no need to do so.

'The plan, then, was this. On Tuesday morning, early, Mottram was to set out for the gorge. Almost immediately afterwards, Brinkman was to take out the motor, as if to go to Pullford. He was to pick up Mottram, who would hide under the seat or disguise himself, or smuggle himself away somehow, and drive like mad for the coast. Later, you, my Lord, would come to the "Load of Mischief", and would get the message about going out to join Mottram at the Long Pool. In passing through the gorge, you would (I fancy) have found some traces there – Mottram's hat, for example, or his fishing-rod; and your first thought would have been that the poor fellow had slipped in. Then, looking round, you would find this letter half-concealed on a high ledge. You would read it, and you would think that Mottram had committed suicide.

'And then – then you would either make the contents of this letter public, or you wouldn't. If Brinkman was right in his estimate, you would keep the letter dark; the death, before long, would be presumed. The Indescribable Company would have been on the point of paying out the halfmillion, when – Mottram would have reappeared, and your Lordship would have been in a delicate position. If Mottram was right in his view of your character, then you would produce the letter; Mottram's death would be regarded as suicide, and the Indescribable would refuse all claims. Then Mottram would have reappeared, and would have seen to it that, in one way or another, the Pullford diocese should be rewarded for the honesty of its Bishop.

'He was not really a very complete conspirator, poor Mottram. He made three bad mistakes, as it proved. Though indeed, they would not have mattered, or two of them would not have mattered, if events had proceeded according to plan.

'In the first place, he went and wrote his name in the

176

Visitors' Book immediately on arrival. He wanted to leave no doubt that it was Jephthah Mottram in person, who arrived at the "Load of Mischief" on Monday night. He wanted journalists to come down here, and look reverently at the great man's signature. Of course, in reality, it is a thing nobody ever does, on the night of arrival. It has made me suspicious from the very first, as my wife will tell you.

'In the second place, when he took the precaution of drawing up a new will, he neglected to sign it overnight. Brinkman, I suppose, pointed out to him that, if any fatal accident occurred – say a motor accident – the codicil leaving the half-million to the Bishop would be perfectly valid, To avoid this danger, they must have drawn up a new will, and if Mottram had signed this overnight, his death would have made it valid. As it was, for some reason – probably because Brinkman himself was drawing it up (I think the writing is Brinkman's) late on Monday night, the will was never signed, and was useless.

'In the third place, he did something overnight which he ought to have left till the next morning. He not only wrote his confidential letter to the Bishop, but he went out with Brinkman to the gorge and posted it – put it on the ledge ready for the Bishop to find it next morning. He did not mean to go into the gorge at all the next morning. He would start out on the way to it, say, at eight, and at ten minutes past eight Brinkman, driving the car, would pick him up on the road. From the side of the road they could throw over Mottram's hat, possibly, and they could slide his rod down the rocks, so as to make it appear that he had been there. (Brinkman, in this way, would establish an *alibi*; he could not be supposed to have murdered Mottram in the gorge.) But it was not safe to let the letter drop in this casual way; therefore the letter must be planted out overnight. There was no great danger of its premature discovery; in any case, Mottram put it rather out of sight, on a ledge so high up that only a tall man would see it, and only if he was looking about him carefully.

'That is the complicated part of this business; the rest of it depends on two simple accidents. Mottram went to bed rather early; he was in an excited frame of mind, and determined to steady himself with a sleeping-draught. The watch, the studs were only symptoms of that fussiness we all feel on the eve of a great adventure. I suppose he borrowed a match from Brinkman to light his gas with. But it was a clear night; there was no need of light to go to bed by. But just at the last moment – a fatal moment for himself – he did light the gas; perhaps he wanted to read a page or two of his novel before turning in.

'The rest of the story could be more easily told upstairs. I wonder if you would mind all coming up into the actual room? It makes it so much easier to construct the scene if you are on the spot.'

The whole party applauded this decision.

'This is what is called an object-lesson, in the education of the young,' observed Mr Pulteney. 'The young like it; they are in a position to hack one another's shins when the teacher's back is turned.'

When they reached the bedroom, Bredon found himself falling into the attitude of a lecturer. 'The guide,' murmured Angela, 'taking a party round the ruins of the old dungeon. Scene of the 'orrible crime. Please pay attention, gentlemen.'

'You see how the gas works in here,' went on Bredon. 'There's the main tap, we'll call it A, which controls the whole supply. Tap B is for the bracket; tap C leads through the tube to the standard lamp. It doesn't matter leaving tap B or tap C on as long as tap A is turned off.

'When Mottram went up to bed, tap B and tap C were both open, but tap A was properly turned off. Mottram took no particular notice of the disposition of taps; he turned on one tap at random, tap A. Then he lit his match, and put it to the bracket, which naturally lit. He then immediately threw the match away. We know that, because we found the match, and it was hardly burned down the stalk at all. Meanwhile, of course, he had also allowed the gas to escape through the tube into the standard lamp; it never occurred to him to light this. The standard was at the other end of the room, close to the open window; the slight escape of gas did not, unfortunately for him, offend his nostrils. Brinkman told me, and it is probably true, that Mottram had not a very keen sense of smell. After a minute or two, feeling ready to go to sleep, he went up to the taps again, and forgot to reverse the process he had gone through before. Instead of turning off the main tap A, he carelessly turned off tap B. And the light on the bracket obediently went out.

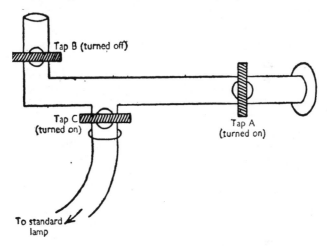

Tap B (turned off)

Tap C (turned on)

Tap A (turned on)

To standard lamp

THE THREE TAPS AS BRINKMAN FOUND THEM

'That is the lesson of the finger-print. Tap A was stiff, and Mottram left a mark when he turned it on; he would have left another if he had turned it off. He did not; he turned off tap B, which works at a mere touch, and of course he left no mark in doing so. There, then, lies Mottram; the sleeping-draught has already taken effect; the wind gets up, and blows the window to; tap A is still open, and tap C is still open; and through the burner of the standard lamp the acetylene is pouring into the room.

'Brinkman is not a late sleeper. The Boots, who is the earliest riser in this establishment, tells me that Brinkman was always awake when he went round for the shoes. On Tuesday morning, Brinkman must have woken early, to be greeted by a smell of gas. It may have crept in through his window, or even come up through the floor, for the floors here are full of cracks. Once he had satisfied himself that the escape was not in his own room, he must have thought of the room below. When he reached the lower passage, the increasing smell of gas left him in no doubt. He knocked at Mottram's door, got no answer, and rushed in, going straight across and opening the window so as to get some air. Then he had time to turn round and see what was on the bed. There was no doubt that he was too late to help.'

'Did he know it was accident?' asked Eames. 'Or did he think it was suicide?'

'I think he must have known it was accident. And now, consider his position. Here was Mottram, dead by accident. There, up in London, was Mottram's codicil, willing half a million to the diocese of Pullford. And that codicil had not been meant to become operative. It had been made only for the purpose of the test. And now, through this accident, the codicil, which did not represent Mottram's real wishes, had suddenly become valid. It would certainly be judged valid, unless – unless the claim were dismissed owing to a verdict of suicide. Brinkman may or may not have been a good man; he was certainly a good secretary. Put yourself in his position, Mr Eames. He could only give effect to his dead master's real wishes by pretending that his dead master had committed suicide.

'You remember the remark in "The Importance of being Earnest", that to lose one parent may be an accident, to lose both looks like carelessness? So it was with Mottram and the taps. Two taps turned on meant, and would be understood to mean, an accident. *But if all three taps were found on, it would look like suicide.* Brinkman acted on the spur of the moment; he was in a hurry, for the atmosphere of the room was still deadly. He wrapped his handkerchief round his fingers, so as to leave no mark. Then in his confusion, *he turned the wrong tap*. He meant to turn tap B on; instead, he turned tap A off. That sounds impossible, I know. But you will notice that whereas tap A and tap B are turned off when they are at the horizontal, tap C is turned off when it is at the vertical. When Brinkman, then, saw the three taps, B and C were both horizontal, and A was vertical, it was natural, in the furry of the moment, for him to imagine that if all three taps were in the same position, that is, all horizontal, they would all be turned on. Instinctively, then, he turned tap A from the vertical to the horizontal. And in doing so, he left the whole three in the same position in which they were before Mottram lit his match. No gas was escaping at all. The result of Brinkman's action was not to corroborate the theory of suicide, but to introduce a quite new theory – that of murder. Half-stifled, he rushed from the room, locked the door on the outside, and took the key away with him up to his room.'

'Steady on,' put in Angela, 'why did he lock the door?'

'It may have been only so as to keep the room private till he had thought the thing out, and the Boots may have come round too soon for him. Or, more probably, it was another deliberate effort to encourage the idea of suicide. Anyhow, his actions from that moment onwards were perfectly clear-headed. He helped to break down the door, and, while Ferrers was examining the gas, while the Boots was lighting a match, he thrust the key in on the inner side of the door. It was only when he had done this, when he thought that he had made the suicide theory an absolute certainty, that he was suddenly confronted with the horrible mistake he had made in turning the wrong tap. It was a bad moment for him, but fortunately one which excused a certain display of emotion.'

'And he thought he would be run in for the murder?' asked Leyland.

'Not necessarily. But your arrival worried him badly; you got hold of the murder idea from the start.'

'Why didn't he skip, then? There was the car, all ready provisioned.'

'The trouble is that Brinkman is, according to his lights, an honest man. And he hated the idea of the Euthanasia money going to the Bishop. I was a godsend to him; here was a nice, stupid man, briefed to defend the thesis of suicide. As soon as I came, he tried to take me out for a walk in the gorge.'

'Why in the gorge?' asked the Bishop.

'So that I should find the letter. Yesterday he did manage to take me to the gorge, and actually drew my

181

attention to the ledge. I saw a bit of paper there, but it never occurred to me to wonder what it was. Poor Brinkman! He must have thought me an ass!'

'But why didn't he get the letter himself, and bring it to us? Or leave it lying about?'

'That was the maddening thing; the poor little man just couldn't reach it. The wind of Monday night had blown it a bit further away, I suspect. Of course, he could have gone out with a step-ladder, or rolled stones up to stand on. But, you see, you were watching him, and I'm pretty sure he knew you were watching him. He thought it best to lead us on, lead me on rather, and make me find out the envelope for myself. When he'd drawn me right across the trail of it, and I'd failed to see it, he was in despair. He decided that he must bolt after all. It was too horrible a position to be here under observation, and fearing arrest at any moment. If he were arrested, you see, he must either tell a lie, and land himself in suspicion, or tell the truth, and see the Euthanasia money fall into Catholic hands.

'He ordered a car from the garage to meet the train which arrives at Chilthorpe at 8.40. He determined to meet it on the way to the station. I don't think the thought of the car lying at the garage, with the sangwiches – I mean the sandwiches – and the whisky on board, occurred to him for a moment. He is an honest man. But on his way to meet the car he would go through the gorge, and make sure that he was followed; he would draw attention to the document, and then disappear from the scene. He had not much luggage; he had only to clear up a few papers, mostly belonging to Mottram. Among these was the unsigned will which had been drawn up, ready for Mottram's signature, on the Monday night. This he burned; it could be no use to anybody now. He burned it standing at the window, and the last, unburnt piece escaped from his fingers, and fluttered down through a second window into the room below – this room, which had been Mottram's. That was your find, Leyland. And the odd thing is, that it was through this absurd detail that I got on to the track of the whole thing. Because one of my patience-cards fluttered down through a groundfloor window; and as I was carrying it upstairs I realized that was how the scrap of paper came to be lying about in Mottram's room. Then I began wondering what the will was, and why Brinkman should have been burning it, and suddenly the whole truth began to sketch itself in on my mind, just as I've been telling it you.

'Brinkman had bad luck to the last. I dropped that card just after he started out with his dispatch-box; he saw that I'd disappeared from the window, and supposed, with delight, that I was following him. With delight, for of course I was the one man who was interested in proving the death to be suicide. He went back to the cache in the gorge, leading me (as he supposed) all the way; then he waited for a flash of lightning, and jumped up so as to draw attention to the envelope. As he came down again he looked round, and, in the last rays of the lightning flash, saw that it was Eames, not I, who was following him. Eames – the one man who would certainly make away with the precious document! But there was no time to be lost; he could hear the taxi already on the hill. He ran round to the road, leaped on board the taxi, and, in desperation, sent a note to me by the taxi-man telling me to make Eames show me what he had found. I don't know where Brinkman is now, but I rather hope he gets clear.'

'Amen to that,' said Leyland; 'it would be uncommonly awkward for us if we found him. What on earth could we charge him with? You can't hang a man for turning the wrong gas-tap by mistake.'

'Poor Mr Simmonds will be relieved about this,' said Angela.

'By the way,' said the Bishop, 'I hear that Mottram did leave some unsettled estate after all, and that, I suppose, will go to Simmonds. Not a great deal, but it's enough for him to marry on.'

Angela swears that at this point she heard, on the other side of the door, a scuffle and the rustle of departing footsteps. She says you can't cure maids of their bad habits, really.

'My own difficulty,' said the Bishop, 'is about my moral claim to this money. For it was left to me, it seems, by a will which the testator did not mean to take effect.'

183

'On the other hand you've earned it, my Lord,' suggested Bredon. 'After all, poor Mottram was only waiting to find out whether you would prove to be an honest man or not. And I think you've come very well out of the test. Besides, you can't refuse the legacy; it's in trust for the diocese. I hope Pullford will see a lot of Catholic activity now.'

'The Church collections will be beginning to fall off almost at once,' said Eames, with a melancholy face.

'I wish I had scrutinized those motor-cushions more closely,' said Mr Pulteney. 'It seems to me that I get nothing out of all this.'

'Which reminds me,' said Leyland, 'I suppose the bet's off.'

'And Mr Bredon,' added the Bishop, 'will get no thanks from his Company. I'm afraid, Mr Bredon, you will have carried nothing away with you from your visit to these parts.'

'Oh, I don't know about that,' said Bredon.

>>> If you've enjoyed this book and would like to discover more great vintage crime and thriller titles, as well as the most exciting crime and thriller authors writing today, visit: >>>

The Murder Room
Where Criminal Minds Meet

themurderroom.com